MAKER

A Valmenessian Novella

Rebecca Camm

Find me at: www.rebeccacamm.com
Instagram: @readingwritingdaydreaming
TikTok: @readingwritingdaydream
Facebook: @readingwritingdaydreaming

Paperback ISBN: 978-0-6453455-7-5

Editor; Emily Morrison
Cover; Artscandare Book Cover Design
Formatter; Rebecca Camm

This book is written in British English.

The Valmenessian Chronicles

Alta: A Valmenessian Novella

Liars and Light

Rise and Reverence

Maker: A Valmenessian Novella

Vice and Verity

Content Notes
Maker is an adult fantasy novella. It contains cursing, sexual
references, violence, and other adult themes.
A full list can be found on my website, rebeccacamm.com
or by scanning the QR code below.

Valmenessia

The Frozen Sea

Kishton

The Great
Northern Forest

Sailor's Peril

Emperor's
Edge

The Mines

Sooby

The Perisyion
Mountains

Milkheaven

Gremlin Woods

Chumley

Pellion

Glitmab

Blessed Reef

Royal
Bay

Ocean's Harbour

Bayton

Desert Harbour

Parkton

The Dividing Waters

1

"Melanie is missing."

"What?" Sloane asked, dropping the papers she'd been holding. They fell to the floor and scattered at her feet, forgotten as she turned to face Annabelle. The woman had been working for Sloane's father for the last ten years, and, in a way, she was like a big sister or young aunt of sorts. "What happened?"

"My neighbour is friends with the guard that attended her home early this morning," Annabelle replied, coming to stand beside her at the counter. Her brown, loosely curled hair swayed along her back from where it was tied into a low ponytail. "Said Melanie had up and left her husband and children in the middle of the night. She'd taken nothing with her, just vanished in her desperation to leave." Annabelle shook her head as she began wrapping dried lavender stems in cloth. "Her husband is distraught, and so are their children."

Working at her father's apothecary gave Sloane Maker

access to all the newest gossip in the city of Devotion. Not necessarily because she was keen to know about the lives of those who resided in the same city as her, but rather that Annabelle was a wonderous gossip who spent her days filling Sloane in on the latest news. Today's announcement, however, Sloane felt compelled to hear. Melanie liked to believe she had magic like those in Valmenessia. It was impossible, of course, but that didn't stop her beliefs. She was a regular customer, always coming in to purchase items for her 'spells'. Sloane had started to like the woman and her eccentric nature over the years, so it was a shock to believe she'd disappeared in the dead of night.

"She could have been kidnapped. Did the guard think that was a possibility?"

"Not that I was told."

"Of course not," Sloane said, kneeling to collect her papers. "Why do they always jump to conclusions that paint women in a horrible light? She could be in danger."

"Nothing dangerous ever happens in Devotion, you know that," Annabelle said. "There are no murders; rarely a crime ever takes place. So the likelihood of a kidnapping is slim."

"But she was fiercely in love with her husband." Sloane frowned, recalling her memories of Melanie. "Not to mention how she felt about her children."

"Perhaps she deceived them. Deceived us all," Annabelle replied with a heavy sigh. "You never really know what goes on in someone else's mind, and that woman had a lot of strange things happening in hers."

Sloane paused, tilting her head to one side. "Maybe he killed her. Buried her body somewhere no one would find."

"That's an awful thing to suggest!" Annabelle exclaimed, slapping her hand on the counter. "Don't say things like that."

"It would be even more awful if we discovered that it was true," Sloane mumbled to herself and hurried with her papers.

"It is such a tragedy, and now her parents must bear the

burden of a daughter who has abandoned her family. Imagine how that's going to look."

"Last I checked, they can't see into the future. There's no way they could have known," Sloane replied. "And we don't know for certain she ran away anyway. There has to be more going on."

"Time will tell. Until then, they will be the talk of the city. I guess we all have our troubles to carry," Annabelle said, blowing her fringe from her freckled forehead and clutching her chest. "You have yours, and I have this wretched heart that bleeds for anyone worse off than me."

"A little dramatic, don't you think?" Sloane said, rising to her feet. Annabelle's first words were true; everyone did have something weighing them down. But the part about her heart bleeding for others was a bit of a stretch. It wasn't that Annabelle had no compassion; it was that her priorities were gossip first and feelings second. "I don't think you should spread gossip about her abandoning her family until we know for sure. Of course, I hope you're right, and she has just run away, but even then, she may have a good reason."

Annabelle bent, her ass high in the air as she sifted through the shelving below the bench. "I'm hardly gossiping, though you're youth makes you so naïve, Sloane. Always wanting to see the best in people."

"I'm twenty-one now, thank you very much," Sloane replied, sticking out her tongue and knowing full well that if Annabelle had been looking, she would have partially proved the woman's point. "And I, for one, would still like to believe in a person's innocence until proven otherwise. You say she ran away and left her family, but did you ever hear her or anyone else say she was unhappy? I definitely never did."

"Hmm," Annabelle replied as she stood. She placed a fresh bundle of cloth on the bench before tapping her lips with a single finger. "No."

"So, ask yourself, why would a happy woman leave her family?" Sloane raised a brow; she knew she had the woman.

Annabelle pursed her lips.

"See!" Sloane threw her hands in the air. "There you go!"

"Where are you going?" came a familiar voice, along with the chiming of the bell that hung at the top corner of the door.

Sloane turned to see Rian stride into the store carrying a wooden crate, causing her to instantly think of mornings. His dark brown hair was short but tousled as though he had gotten out of bed only moments ago, and his eyes reminded her of maple syrup-smothered pancakes.

"To Valmenessia," Sloane replied, grinning mischievously. She pushed the loose strands of her silver-blonde hair from her face and tucked them behind her ear. "Annabelle is running away with a handsome Lys Alv with long flowing blond hair and rock-hard abs, who likes to serenade her through song."

"Sexy accent? Likes to speak in metaphors?" Rian asked as he placed his delivery on the floor before the counter. He was a tall man with broad shoulders and muscular legs from all the manual labour involved in making deliveries around the city.

Sloane nodded, looking up at him.

"I always knew you were the wild romantic type, Annabelle," he teased.

"The wildest," Sloane wiggled her brows. "You should hear her stories. Real minx."

"You two aren't funny," Annabelle sang, coming around the counter to stand beside Rian as he laughed with Sloane.

"I like to think we are funny," Sloane said with a pout.

"Well, hate to break it to you, but you're not," Annabelle said, bending to inspect the supplies he'd brought. "What have you brought today?"

"Only a small delivery," he said, smiling at Sloane, a dimple appearing on one of his cheeks. "Some garlic and witch hazel."

"Oh good," Annabelle said, straightening. "We were running

low on those."

Despite Annabelle being a renowned gossip, as far as Sloane knew, she hadn't told a soul of the true goings on at the apothecary, not even Rian. Sloane's father technically ran the apothecary, yet he hadn't been mixing remedies for well over a year. Sloane had been taking on his role, though she tried to keep that knowledge a secret in front of customers and, in this case, delivery men; it still surprised her that Annabelle hadn't let it slip.

The city of Devotion would not have approved of a young woman creating their remedies. In some ways, her home was progressive, the fact that it was not expected for women to marry early or at all, but when it came to things like law, politics, business and healthcare, they were a man's job. She didn't think Rian would disapprove of her running the apothecary, but letting more people in on the secret was a surefire way of having everyone find out. Annabelle knew because she worked there, and the only other person Sloane had told was Emma, but best friends were supposed to keep secrets.

Sloane's father could not do much these days, let alone run the apothecary. His obsession with their family history, combined with his night terrors, was all he could handle.

He spent his days rereading books that had been passed down through the generations, sometimes enacting rituals that were written on the pages, other times reciting passages until he knew them by heart. His interest had become all-consuming to the point that he no longer left their home, even for work.

During the day, his emotions were mild, and his manner was that of a man purely interested in broadening his knowledge base on a topic he found interesting. At night, however, her father's mind was a contrast that Sloane found frightening.

He would wake in the middle of the night, shouting and tearing apart his room. His cries were not anger but grief, which was evident by the tears on his face and the words that would leave his lips, begging for the return of his love. It broke Sloane's heart every night to see him that way, deep in sleep, yet with his emotions on display, revealing the depths of his loss.

A loss that she had caused.

"Everything alright?" Rian asked, drawing her attention back to the present. His eyes were fixed intently on her face as he leant towards her. "Lost in thought?"

"Yeah, I'm fine," Sloane replied. She closed her eyes, breathed in deeply, and then offered him a tight-lipped smile before voicing a lie. "I was thinking about everything I have to do around here … and Melanie."

Rian straightened though the expression on his face made her think that he wasn't convinced by the lie she'd told. They had known each other since they were children when Rian would accompany his father on deliveries. At one point, she had had the misconceived idea that they would fall in love and marry, especially when she'd started to notice how handsome he was becoming, but he'd never shown an interest in her in that way, and the fantasy had vanished. Maybe it was due to him being a few years older than her; she hadn't dwelled on it. Now, all she saw standing before her was a good friend.

He ran a hand through his hair, which was long enough on top to fall onto his forehead when he looked down. "I heard. Were you friends?"

"I wouldn't say we were close," Sloane shook her head. "But she came in here a lot, and I liked her. I still like her."

"I'm sure—"

"Sloane, there is a lot to be done," Annabelle interrupted, then nodded towards Rian. "You must have a busy day ahead too."

"Right. Not the subtlest of hints," he chuckled. "I believe that is my cue to leave you to it, then."

"I'll go with you," Sloane said. "I mean, I'm not helping you with your deliveries, but I'll walk with you out. I have some errands to run."

Rian held the door open for her, and she stepped onto the dirt road. The day was sunny for Harvest Season, though a cool breeze blew through the air, a reminder to the citizens that Frost Season had only just passed. Shops and other small businesses lined the street selling items from clothing to furnishings as well as services like blacksmithing.

"How are my other orders?" she asked, walking with Rian towards his wagon. It was piled high with boxes and baskets filled with goods for those all around the city. It needed a good clean and a fresh coat of paint, and there used to be a name painted on the side when Rian's father had taken care of the deliveries, but now all that was legible was the letter H.

Sloane walked past the wagon, straight to the sooty grey horse that pulled it along. She lifted a hand, and the horse nudged its head into her palm, eager for her pats.

"I should have the cloth to you before the end of next week," Rian said. He stood beside her and reached out, running his hand down the horse's mane. "If Hawk had his way, I'd be here every hour."

"What's the point in being friends if I don't get speedy deliveries?" Sloane teased.

"You get someone to help you mess with Annabelle," he grinned. "Also, I'm here every day, which is more often than any other customer."

She laughed, tilting her head his way to see that Rian was watching her, not the horse as she had thought. He was standing much closer too. He looked down at her and smiled.

"Well, Hawk is a sucker for pats, and I'm inclined to give into him," she said, turning to face the horse as a flush of heat crept up her neck. "So I guess that's a benefit too."

"Look, two benefits. Lucky girl," Rian chuckled. "I also spoke to the chandler yesterday, and he said they are almost complete."

"Tell him to hurry up," Sloane said, stepping back. She

smiled as she walked backwards down the street. Rian was such a good friend; she loved how easy their relationship was and how he had the uncanny ability to always make her smile. "I only have a few more days' supply; then I'll be in trouble. How am I supposed to get dressed in the dark?"

Rian laughed. "I'll be sure to let him know you'll struggle to put clothes on without the candles. Not sure it will make him hurry, though."

"Oh shit!" Sloane blushed. She hadn't meant for her words to come out like that. "That's not what I meant!"

"Sure it wasn't." Rian winked.

"Just tell him to hurry up!" she called, before turning away to stop embarrassing herself any more than she already had.

2

The sun was setting in the west, casting the late afternoon in an angry orange glow. It was as though it was outraged at the idea of having to disappear beyond the horizon and give the moon a chance to glow in the sky. Sloane couldn't blame it; she'd be pissed off, too, if she had to miss the dance at Walsh Manor.

"You should come," Sloane said, turning her attention from the sun's last dying rays falling on the rolling hills to look at her father, who was sitting in his favourite armchair with a candle burning brightly on the table beside him. They lived above the apothecary in a small but modest home. "The new lord is back, and apparently, he has brought friends with him."

"My love," her father began without looking up from the page he was reading though she would bet a handful of coins that he had memorised the page months ago. His hair was darker than hers, more of a yellow blond, and he had a thin frame which had become to look less merely thin and more ill after he decided not to leave the house. "I have told you before. Attending events gives people the impression that I am looking for a partner."

Sloane sighed. "No, it gives them the impression that you are alive."

He licked the tips of his fingers and turned the page. "They would know if I died."

"Would they?" She said exasperatedly. "No one has seen you in an eternity. For all I know, you are a ghost haunting me."

"That's a bit dramatic," he said with a chuckle. He glanced over the pages, taking her in with his deep blue eyes. "You don't need me to hold your hand. I raised you to be independent."

"Yes, but even independent people want their fathers to go with them to do fun things now and again."

"I'm sorry, but I can't."

Sloane chewed her lip. "Would it be so bad if you were to meet someone?"

"Makers love once, Sloane," he said, his words clipped. "You know that. Now, what time is Emma due?"

Her friend was coming to collect Sloane in one of her family carriages. Sloane and her father were neither poor nor rolling in coins. They didn't have a horse, never needing one, and so they didn't have a carriage either. Everywhere they needed to travel was within walking distance, so a carriage was unnecessary; at least, that's what her father believed.

"She should be here any minute," Sloane replied, deciding not to press her father on his shitty excuse any further. It was a waste of breath. He would never change his mind. He was devoted to her mother, even if it had been twenty-one years since she passed.

The day Sloane took her first breath, her mother had taken her last.

"Don't be late home," her father said.

"Wouldn't dream of being late," she replied with a grin. "Though would you come to get me if I was?"

"No," he said with a chuckle. "It's not a rule, only advice. You'll regret it in the morning when you wake up tired for work."

"Why can't you be like normal parents?"

"You want me to force you to my will?" he asked with a shake of his head. "I'm afraid I can't do that. You are not mine to control. You are your own person and an adult now too. It is important for you to make your own choices in life and deal with the outcomes."

"So you want me to walk the world alone and ignorant?"

"You are far from ignorant," he said. "And you are not alone. Emma will be with you. As for the dramatics of walking the entire world, I am here and will always be here for you."

Sloane frowned. "Come with me."

"Sloane..." he groaned as the sound of hoof beats came from outside.

"Fine. Don't wait up for me," she said, hurrying over to her father and kissing him on the cheek. The man grumbled about not making promises. But she didn't stop to reply, gathering her skirts, and dashed downstairs and out the door.

Her father may not have wanted to go out, but luckily, Sloane had never had to attend a dance alone. Emma had always made sure to collect her for any event, and even though she wished for her father to have more of a social life, she wouldn't trade all the wonderful memories she now had of the fun times with her best friend.

The driver opened the carriage door and offered a hand, helping Sloane inside, where she found her friend nose-deep in a book.

"No, nope, not happening," Sloane said, snatching the book from Emma's grasp. "I just had to have a conversation with my father while he simultaneously read. I'm not doing that with you."

Emma laughed, reaching out as she swayed with the motion of the carriage beginning to move along the dirt road. "Fine, but let me at least keep it for later."

"Does your father know you have it?" Sloane asked, handing the book over.

"Who do you think gave it to me?" Emma smirked, her brown eyes alight. Cream-coloured powder dusted her eyelids, and a rose tint had been applied to her cheeks. "He said he was sick of me pestering him about the law and decided that I was never going to give up and that giving me a few books would provide him with some peace and quiet—and make me more obedient."

"Obedient?"

"I have a curfew now, and he's adjusting my allowance," she replied, her shoulders sagging. "Oh, and I have to meet with a candidate he thinks would be a good match for me."

Sloane scrunched her nose. She was suddenly grateful that her father didn't have any intentions of inflicting those sorts of rules upon her, despite what she said to him earlier.

"I knew he would expect it of me sooner or later; at least this way, I get something I want in return."

"Does this mean he will let you study at the school?" Sloane raised her brows at her friend. Emma's father was a well-respected lawman in Devotion, and despite the man's frustration towards Emma's interests, he knew his daughter planned on following in his footsteps.

"Of course not," Emma replied. "But I will find a way. If there's something I have learnt over the years, it's that the law has many loopholes, and I plan on exploiting a few."

"I pity anyone who tries to get in your way," Sloane said, and the two women burst into laughter.

Sloane loved that Emma was intent on forging her own path, even though the world insisted she should stick to the one set out before her. Sometimes Sloane wished she was as courageous and confident in her destiny, fighting for possibilities, as Emma.

Possibility was what Emma truly wanted. Yes, she was studying law, but ultimately it was about the chance to be anything her heart desired. Why should men have all the choices and women only a handful?

The carriage joined a line as it slowly moved along the candle-lit path before pulling to a stop before Walsh Manor. It was the largest building in all of Devotion, big enough to fit multiple families. But it was only home to Lady Walsh and her son, the new lord of Devotion, and of course, their staff.

The driver appeared beside the carriage, opening the door and offering a hand for the women to step out. Emma exited first, her pale green, beaded skirt cascading to the stone steps as she climbed out. Her dress was beautiful; the bodice was tight around her waist and sewn with a delicate lace over a fabric that matched the lower half of her ensemble. Emma's light brown hair was up in a plaited sort of crown with small white flowers woven through it. She looked stunning, as usual.

Sloane took the driver's hand and stepped out. Unlike her friend, she did not have as much coin to spend on gowns, so her dress was a simple lilac with minimal frill or embellishments. She had styled her silver-blonde hair by tying half up and letting the rest fall around her shoulders in waves.

The two young women strode up the stairs towards the entrance of Walsh Manor. The Walshs were not only the ruling family of Devotion but the wealthiest in the area as well. Excitement sparked in Sloane at the prospect of a night of dancing, wine and friends. She smiled to herself as they reached the top of the stairs and entered through the ornate front doors.

Servants stood at the doors, greeting the guests as they arrived. Sloane and Emma past them politely and strode on the polished wooden floors of the warmly lit hallway towards the ballroom. Portraits and landscape art lined the walls as they went, catching their eyes. Despite their wealth, or perhaps because of it, the Walsh family opened parts of their home regularly to the people of Devotion for events such as this. Sloane had walked the halls many a time, but each time hadn't diminished the magnificence of the place or the awe she felt in being within its walls.

"I hate this song," Emma said as the music grew louder with each step they took. "I'm glad we missed it."

Sloane laughed. "It's not that bad."

"It's not very good either," came a voice from behind, and both women turned to see two men walking behind them; one wearing black trousers and a coat with a white shirt beneath, the other in a similar ensemble, only he wore navy blue instead of black.

"My lord," Emma said, grabbing Sloane's hand and pulling them both into a curtsey. "Thank you for inviting us to your home."

Lord Walsh had been to boarding school in another city for most of his life and had only returned to Devotion after his father had passed to take up his position as the new lord. Sloane hadn't recognised him looking so much more mature than last she'd seen him, even though it had only been afar. Perhaps it was his new responsibilities as Lord of the house that caused the change in his air.

"I think it should be me thanking you both for taking time out of your busy lives to join us for a dance," he replied smoothly, his grey eyes looking between Sloane and Emma. The young lord smiled broadly, immediately making Sloane feel at ease. "Without the people of Devotion, these events my mother organises would be dull."

"I couldn't imagine any event your mother organises to be anything other than amazing," Sloane said, thinking of all the times she'd been to a Walsh family event.

They had always been full of grandeur; the lady of the family did nothing by halves. Even after the late Lord Walsh passed recently, she was only absent for a few weeks before reassuming her parties. If only Sloane's father would consider stepping back into the social life of Devotion like Lady Walsh instead of delving deeper into their family history.

"I'll have to pass on your compliments, Miss...?" Lord Walsh eyed her expectantly.

"Sloane Maker," she replied with a smile. "And this is my friend Emma Charter."

"It is lovely to meet you both," he said, bowing his head. "This is Nevan Grim. We went to school together."

He gestured to the man in black beside him, not that Sloane needed any direction to spot the lord's friend. Nevan Grim was beyond handsome. He had honey-coloured hair styled to resemble somewhat of a wave, and he smiled warmly, the expression a contrast to the sharp planes of his strong nose and jaw. Though, that was what made Sloane all that more intrigued by him.

Emma reached for Sloane's hand for the second time that night and pulled her into a curtsey, though, unlike the first time, she didn't bow her head, her eyes unable to part with the man's gaze. Instead, she was trapped in his brown eyes, and when he smiled directly at her, her heart skipped a beat in her chest.

Shit. Is this what love at first sight feels like? She wondered. Her father had always said, Makers love once, so she'd expected it to be an overwhelming feeling.

"We should probably head inside," Lord Walsh said once the women stood tall again. He gestured towards the ballroom. "After you, ladies."

Sloane bit her lip and let Emma tug her away. Her feet wouldn't have carried her very far if her friend didn't direct them for her. As they entered the ballroom, they were swept up in the atmosphere of the dance. The music was played by a quartet poised in the far corner, and the melody filled the room, directing those dancing in the centre. Above them, candles flickered in candelabras hung from the roof, illuminating not only the guests who moved gracefully to the song playing but those around the edges laughing and chatting amongst themselves. A long table sat pressed against the nearest wall, delicious-looking dishes spread out amongst its surface and drew in those enticed by the mouth-watering aromas.

"Someone caught your eye," Emma said, leaning into Sloane.

"Was it that obvious?" she groaned.

"Yes!" Emma laughed. "But I think you caught his eye, too, so I wouldn't worry."

"He is well above my social standing," she said as they stopped at the table. Her gaze raked over the spread.

"Who cares?" Emma replied, squeezing Sloane's wrist. "You haven't even spoken to him yet; for all you know, he's handsome with an awful personality."

"True," Sloane smiled, selecting a small fruit tart. "The night has only just begun."

3

Sloane and Emma took in the festivities and greeted
familiar faces, pausing to watch the people dance when
the music changed to a lively tempo. The guests spun
and twirled, keeping pace, and Sloane found herself eager to join
them in the revelries. She loved dancing. The feel of the music
carrying her around a room was as though she were under some
spell put on her by a Conjurer in Valmenessia. Everyone knew
of that distant country and the magic that existed there. And even
though there was no magic beyond the waters of Valmenessia,
Sloane liked to think that music and dancing were pretty close
to it.

"How's your composure?" Emma asked, drawing Sloane's
attention from the dancing. "Because Lord Walsh and his friend
are walking over here."

Sloane ran her hands down her skirts, then relaxed into what
she hoped was an appropriate smile and not some soppy, doe-
eyed expression as the duo approached.

"How is it that you two are not off dancing in the arms of someone yet?" Lord Walsh asked, a hand on his chest as he feigned shock. He offered a hand to Emma. "Help me fix it."

"Bold of you to assume that we are not dancing by choice."

"Is it a choice?"

"It might be."

"Are you choosing to say no now?"

Emma pursed her lips, taking his hand. "I suppose it would be rude to turn down the host."

Lord Walsh led her onto the dance floor, giving Sloane a wink as he did and smiling broadly. Many people were put off by Emma's matter-of-factness, but it appeared the lord enjoyed her attitude.

"Your friend knows her worth," Nevan said, coming to stand by Sloane.

"It's not very appropriate for her to speak to him that way," she said. "He's the lord of the city."

"I'd say that gives her more reason to make Connor work for her attention," Nevan replied, his lips tugging up at one side. "He already has enough people kissing his ass."

Surprised laughter burst from Sloane. "Emma is definitely not the kind of person to bow to just anyone."

"I noticed," Nevan grinned. "What about you?"

"What about me?" Sloane asked.

"Are you a force to be reckoned with too?" Nevan asked with a conspiratorial glint in his eyes.

Sloane shook her head. "I'm definitely the sidekick in this case. Nothing special."

"I'm not so sure about that," he replied, taking her hand and leading her to the dance floor. He spun her around so that they were facing each other, then placed his free hand on her waist, pulling her closer. "I think special is exactly what you are."

The melody changed, and Sloane found herself being twirled around. Her feet moved quickly, recalling the steps she had memorised. At the same time, her heart thumped at a similar pace whenever she found Nevan looking at her. How was it that he had this effect on her? It was as though she had ingested too much milk of the poppy or inhaled mushroom powder and had suddenly lost control of her own mind.

Perhaps she'd accidentally dosed herself today... She'd been working with the last of the mushrooms, creating elixirs earlier that afternoon. There was a chance she hadn't noticed inhaling something or it absorbing through her skin. She would have to be more careful from now on.

"I gather from the compliments you have for Connor's mother," Nevan began, placing the palm of his hand gently against her raised one. The cufflink on his wrist caught the light, and she noticed the sparkle of a gemstone eye inside a black obsidian snake. "That you are a regular at these events."

"Emma and I do attend a few," she replied as they turned in a circle, his eyes never leaving her face. "Not all. I work at my father's apothecary, so I sometimes have to miss out when duty calls."

"Mixing tonics and the like is the closest thing we have to the magic of Valmenessia," he said. "You're like a Conjurer."

Sloane blushed. "I wouldn't go that far."

"Why not?" he asked, stepping to meet her and placing a hand on her waist while the other clasped around her hand. "You manipulate items from the world around you in a specific way to create something new. Isn't that what Conjurers do?"

"I guess," she said, having difficulty coming up with an argument when all she could focus on was the pressure of his hands on her. His thumb was moving up and down as if simply holding her hand was not enough; he needed to caress it too.

He led Sloane into another dance, and she couldn't help the smile that stretched across her face as they moved to the music. She liked that he had chosen her over everyone else and that everyone in the room saw whom she was dancing with.

Her heart beat rapidly in her chest as she stepped out into the night. Her cheeks and feet were sore, the first from smiling so much and the other from dancing for what felt like hours. Out of all the events Sloane had attended, this had been her favourite and would remain in her memories until the day she died.

"I don't think I've danced so much in my life," Nevan said, leaning back against a stone fence and looking to the night sky. "You're something special, you know that?"

"You've only known me a few hours," Sloane replied, heat creeping up her neck.

"Maybe," he said, his gaze catching hers. She froze, completely held by his stare as he stepped towards her. "You don't know how long I have been looking for you." He pushed a strand of her hair behind her ear, causing her to shiver. "I can't believe I've finally found you."

Sloane closed her eyes as he leaned in, anticipation filling her. Everything he was saying felt so right. That they were meant to be.

Their attraction was instant.

Destined.

She pushed up on her toes, ready to feel his lips against hers, only to be pulled to the side by a firm grip.

"We're leaving," Emma announced, dragging Sloane along behind her.

"What? Why?" Sloane asked, trying to gather her thoughts. She glanced back to see Nevan watch her leave with a frown on his face. "Couldn't you see I was in the middle of something?"

"I have a curfew, remember," Emma said breathlessly. "Also, you shouldn't kiss a man like *that* the first time you meet them."

Sloane narrowed her eyes at her friend. "Kiss him like what?"

Emma shook her head. "No, I mean a man like that; rich, powerful, etcetera, etcetera. He's used to getting exactly what he wants. Don't be so easy."

"Excuse me?" Sloane pulled to a stop. "I'm not easy."

Emma looked around, and when she was satisfied there was no one in sight, she placed her hands on her hips. "I'm not trying to be cruel, Sloane. I'm trying to watch out for you. You've never had the attention of someone like him before. You don't know what they are like. Trust me."

"You think I'm beneath him and am stupid enough to fall at his feet."

"No," Emma shook her head. "Okay, he may be above your station, but you're not stupid or beneath him in any way that counts. He is beneath you in that aspect; everyone is. You are at the very top." She offered Sloane a smile and reached out to place a gentle hand on Sloane's arm. "I love you; I want to help you."

Sloane pursed her lips. Emma wasn't usually like this. She was always preaching about women being able to do as they wished. Make their own choices and forge their own paths. Sloane folded her arms over her chest and tapped her foot, looking at her friend expectantly. "What happened with Lord Walsh?"

"Nothing," Emma replied, dropping her gaze.

"So this whole overprotective thing was triggered purely by you caring about me?"

"Okay, fine," Emma sighed heavily. "I do care about you, just so you know, and I meant what I said about watching out for men like him, but my outburst may have had more to do with me than you."

Sloane dropped her arms, softening. "What happened?"

"He asked to court me," Emma blurted out in a rush.

Sloane blinked in surprise. "Lord Walsh wants to court you,

and you're running away?"

"Not running away," she replied. "It's late, and we need to leave anyway because I have a curfew, and you have to work in the morning, and I am being a good friend who cares about your wellbeing. I don't want you to be tired."

"All this intense worry about me," Sloane said, then her brows shot up, realisation dawning on her. "He's the reason your father is letting you read his law books! You've met Lord Walsh before tonight!"

Emma winced. "Only a handful of times. Father had invited Connor over..."

"Connor," Sloane winked, earning a groan from Emma. "Oh shit! I introduced you two like some idiot." She slapped herself on the forehead. "You could have told me you knew him, so I didn't make a fool of myself like that."

"I know," Emma said. She chewed her lip, looking off into the distance. "I ... I wanted to pretend like it wasn't real. Telling you makes it real."

"You don't want him to court you?"

"I honestly don't know. I mean, he seems nice, and we get along well. It's just that in the back of my mind, all I can think of is how our courting was arranged. And if we do marry, it was all set up. Our parents had organised the whole thing before Connor's father died." Emma frowned. "I wanted to be with someone because I fell in love."

"What makes you think you won't fall in love with Lord Walsh? Just because you were introduced by your father doesn't mean it can't be real," Sloane said. She stepped forward, pulling Emma into a hug. "We were introduced to each other by our parents, and my love for you is real."

Emma huffed a laugh.

"You're overthinking it," Sloane said, pulling back to look into her friend's eyes. "Did you say yes?"

"I didn't," she replied. "But I didn't say no either. Just sort of mumbled an excuse and left."

"Okay, so you haven't committed to anything. You have time to think about it."

"What if he doesn't ask again?" Emma grumbled, her shoulders slumping. "What if I've ruined it?"

"Let's not worry about that now," Sloane said, offering her friend a warm smile. "It's late. All this can be tomorrow's problem."

"Alright," Emma nodded firmly. "Tomorrow's problem."

4

S loane found herself barely able to pay attention to the
customer before her—her mind still lost in the dance
from the other night. She always had fun when out
with Emma, but Nevan Grim had made that particular evening
stand out. They had danced all night, he was so handsome, and
luckily he had a good personality too. She'd only ever thought
about Rian when it came to marriage and children, but that was
when she was younger. When those daydreams fizzled, there
hadn't been another to catch her attention until now. Nevan was
unlike anyone she'd ever met, and she couldn't believe that he
had refused other offers and insisted on dancing with her for the
entire evening. He'd completely taken hold of her thoughts.

"Sloane," the older woman before her said. "My headache?"

"Oh, yes, right," Sloane replied. She stopped twirling her
fingers through the end of her ponytail and quickly reached for
the peppermint oil. "Massage a small amount into your temples.
It will ease the pain. And make sure you are drinking plenty of

water."

"Thank you," the woman said, taking the small bottle, then repeated Sloane's instructions back.

"Exactly," Sloane nodded. "Now, if you take it to the counter, Annabelle will sort out payment," she said with a smile, her mind eager to return to her memories and the man who occupied them.

Sloane had danced so much that her feet still ached where she'd developed a couple of nasty blisters. But there was no way she would voice a complaint about them. They were worth it and nothing a salve couldn't ease. So she'd suck it up, especially as she was due to go foraging for mushrooms with Emma soon.

Smiling, Sloane moved through the shelves, finding what she was looking for amongst the array of remedies, and was about to step into the back room when Annabelle called for her.

"Sloane! Sloane!"

"Mmm?" she replied, pausing to see Annabelle waving. Her loose floral sleeves swished with the exaggerated movement. "I'm just going to put this on my feet before I go."

"Wait! A package arrived for you."

Sloane raised a brow, forgetting her feet, and strode over to the counter. "From who?"

"No idea," Annabelle replied, holding out a small box.

She took it, carefully opening the lid to reveal a golden key attached to a chain within. The detail was exquisite. As she picked it up, the key glimmered in the light.

"What is it?" Annabelle asked, leaning over the counter. "A key!"

"Who left it?" Sloane scrunched her brow, looking around the apothecary, but there was no one else in the shop other than the two of them. Beyond the windows, townsfolk were striding passed, and no one looked overly familiar or out of place.

Annabelle shook her head. "It was a delivery boy; I doubt a ten-year-old is sending you gifts like that. I wonder what it unlocks."

"And he didn't say—"

"Not a word about who it's from."

Sloane stared at the key before her, admiring the intricate design. It was beautiful, more beautiful than a key needed to be. Her heart hammered within her as she carefully examined it; it must have cost a fortune for the gold, not to mention having someone craft it too.

"This is so romantic," Annabelle sighed, leaning her hip on the counter. "A secret admirer."

"I'm not so sure it's a secret," Sloane replied, immediately thinking of Nevan. There was only one person she knew who could afford something like it. The key must have been from Nevan Grim because who else would send something like it to her? "I think I know who it's from."

"Who?" Annabelle asked. She almost dove over the counter in her eagerness to hear who had sent it.

"I'm not saying," Sloane said, placing the key back in its box. "If he wanted everyone to know, he would have delivered it himself or at least left a card with his name."

"So you're planning on torturing me?" Annabelle said with an exasperated sigh. "Can't you give me a hint?"

Sloane shook her head; a smile spread across her face. It must plague such a gossip to be left out of the loop.

"You better get out of here then, or I will have to think of some creative ways of getting the information from you."

Sloane laughed. "I'm going," Sloane laughed, striding towards the counter, not bothering to put salve on her feet anymore. Annabelle was right. She was running late. She grabbed her bag, slinging it over her shoulder, and collected the package with the key inside. "The mushrooms aren't going to pick themselves."

Leaving the apothecary, Sloane made her way through the city. It wasn't the biggest, with many of the closest cities boasting double, if not triple, the populations. Wagons rolled along the dirt road, and people maneuvered around them, eager to reach their destinations.

Sloane quickened her pace, conscious of the time, and made her way towards Emma's home. Her friend's family lived in the main city, their home a double-storey stone building that displayed the family's power within Devotion. People sought the services of Emma's father, his knowledge of the law aiding in various issues as long as they paid his fees.

Whilst Lord Walsh lived in a manor outside of the city, the rest of the wealthy resided within the bustle. Their coin meant they did not need to own land for crops or livestock, as they simply had their produce delivered directly to their staffed kitchens. Most of the population resided beyond the main city, with small plots of land sustaining their families.

Sloane had been told of the Elementum in Valmenessia, who could assist the growth of fruits and vegetables and provide an abundance of food for their cities, thus enabling people to live in all sorts of housing no matter their financial situation.

Unfortunately, the people of Devotion were mere humans and had no such luxuries. Whilst Sloane and her father lived further into the city than most, they had a gated garden behind the apothecary where vegetables grew and chickens roosted. Some of the supplies for their store grew in the garden, but many things needed to be bought or gathered elsewhere, like the mushrooms.

Reaching Emma's home, Sloane clasped her hands around the iron fence and stared up at the building, looking precisely at the window of Emma's bedroom on the second floor. Her best friend sat behind the glass and looked down at Sloane with a smile.

Sloane waved, and Emma disappeared from sight before hurrying out the front door moments later, wearing a simple blue dress and her hair pinned on one side.

"You're late," Emma said breathlessly.

"I know," Sloane replied. "I got caught up."

"With a customer?"

"Yes," Sloane nodded. "But also with this."

She handed the box to Emma as they walked away from the house. They headed west towards the woods that bordered the city.

"What's this?" Emma asked, brows raised as she lifted the lid. She gasped, her gaze darting between Sloane and the key. "It's beautiful! Is this from Nevan?"

"I think so," Sloane grinned. "There was no note, but who else could it be?"

Emma slapped Sloane on the arm. "See, not kissing him has paid off."

"I'm not going to be keeping my distance so he'll give me gifts."

"Obviously," Emma rolled her eyes. "But at least you know he is besotted with you."

Sloane blushed, her step bouncing a little as she walked. It was a strange yet exciting thing to have someone romantically think of her. Not that she thought she was unlovable or anything. Just that such a thing could affect her like it was.

"What about you?" Sloane asked, taking the box back and slipping it away into her bag. "Any news from Lord Walsh?"

"No," Emma said, shaking her head. "Maybe it's a good thing. He's moved on to other options."

"You don't know that for sure. He might be busy. Ruling a city has to fill your days."

"I guess," her friend replied with a shrug. "Anyway, there may be quite a few people vying for his attention, but it's not like I don't have options myself."

Sloane's lips tugged up at one side though she didn't comment. Emma did have options, but she could tell her friend liked the lord, despite having run away from him.

At the city's outskirts, they crossed a small stream and entered the tree line. The temperature dropped, and Sloane was grateful she'd put on the thicker dark purple dress this morning instead of the lighter violet one she'd been contemplating. They ventured through the underbrush, their gazes fixed on the ground as they searched for mushrooms.

"How is your father?" Emma asked, picking a large common mushroom from the ground. "Still won't come out of the house?"

"Nope," Sloane replied. "Other than venturing into the garden to pick vegetables or collect eggs, he has no contact with the outside world beyond me."

"I guess he can see people through the windows or the fence pickets; maybe that helps him keep his sanity."

"I have a feeling it's already lost to him," Sloane said, searching around a fallen tree trunk. "He's so obsessed with our family history. He's currently copying old books into new ones. He's desperate to preserve what's written there."

"It must be important."

"They're just old journals. Great grandmothers and grandfathers writing about their boring days," Sloane cleared her throat. " 'Today, I milked the cow and picked some carrots. Tomorrow I will do the same.' "

Emma laughed. "Your ancestors lived exciting lives."

"We weren't anything special," Sloane shrugged as they delved deeper into the woods. "Keeping records of the mundane is pointless. My father is wasting his life."

"Maybe, but at least it gives you some independence. You are in charge of the apothecary."

"Not that anyone knows beyond you and Annabelle. As far as the citizens of Devotion are concerned, my father is merely too busy to see people now, and I am his errand girl."

"You are far more than an errand girl."

Sloane sighed. "Again, you see it, but that doesn't mean anyone else does."

"I guess it's the same as how you *see* me," Emma said, and Sloane looked over to her friend to see her smiling broadly. "True friendship right there."

"Were you doubting it?" Sloane teased, her lips quirking at one side.

The sound of dogs barking echoed through the woods, and Sloane turned, her gaze searching for the source.

"Someone out for a walk?" Emma asked, coming to stand beside her.

"Maybe—" Sloane began only to halt her words at the sound of shouting joining the barking, then all of a sudden, an arrow flew through the trees, penetrating a nearby trunk. She faced Emma, her brows high. "Hunting party."

The women dropped to a crouch, hearts racing as more arrows flew passed.

"Stop!" Emma shouted, cupping her hands around her mouth. "Don't shoot!"

"What are they shooting at?" Sloane asked, turning her head this way and that in search of the hunters' prey. "I can't see a single animal here."

"Stop!" Emma screamed again, but there was no use; more arrows flew. The hunters' shouts grew louder and louder, along with the dog's barking.

"Shit!" Sloane shouted, grabbing Emma's hand and running towards a fallen log.

She dragged her friend to the ground, and they huddled closer to the ground so that they were pressed into the dirt just as a deer ran through the trees. Sloane held her breath as well as Emma's hand as the deer leapt over them and bolted away, arrows chasing after it. The two women waited for whoever was hunting to draw closer, hoping that they would pass and the girls could avoid being shot. Sloane watched the sky, her breaths coming in quick succession, then after a few minutes, when it was quiet, Emma untangled herself from Sloane, rising slowly to her feet.

"I think it's sa—"

One minute Emma was standing there; the next, a whooshing

sound pierced the air, and she fell to the ground, still as the night.

"Emma!" Sloane shouted, diving over her friend. Her eyes were wide as she took in every inch of her friend, searching for the wound from the arrow. "Please, please, please."

Emma started convulsing, and Sloane held back a sob as she looked for where her friend had been hit, her hands running all over Emma's body.

Why couldn't she find the stupid wound?!

5

L aughter burst from Emma's lips, and Sloane froze.

"I got you," Emma said, clutching her stomach. "You should see your face."

Emma's laugh rang out around the woods, but Sloane didn't move; her hands splayed out before her.

It was a joke? A fucking joke?

"You bitch!" Sloane jumped onto Emma, and the two rolled around whilst the former tried to inflict pain, and the latter laughed her heart out.

"I was terrified!" Sloane said, rolling off Emma and falling onto her back. The two women lay side by side on the ground, covered in leaf litter and dirt, trying to catch their breath.

"I know!" Emma replied, her head falling to the side and a huge grin on her face. "It was a bad joke, but I just couldn't resist."

Sloane groaned, elbowing Emma in the side. "You're evil."

Footsteps sounded, and the two women looked up to see

Lord Walsh and Nevan Grim running towards them dressed in caramel brown pants, black coats and shiny knee-high boots.

"I'm sorry," Emma said, frowning at Sloane.

"Are you okay?" Lord Walsh's words fell from him as he descended upon Emma. He looked as panicked as Sloane had been moments ago. He ran a hand over her forehead, sweeping away her fringe. "Where did it hit you?"

"It didn't," Sloane replied stiffly before Emma could. Nevan offered a hand, and she took it, rising from the ground to stand before him. His hand was warm in hers, and she offered him a smile before wiping away the dirt from her dress. Luckily it was a dark colour and would hide much of the mess. "Thank you."

"It missed you? But we saw you fall," Lord Walsh said, looking down at Emma with his brow creased in confusion.

"Connor, I'm fine," Emma said. She sat up, now eye level with the lord and smirked. "You need to work on your aim."

Sloane rolled her eyes. "Have mercy."

"What brings the two of you to the woods?" Nevan asked.

"Picking mushrooms," Sloane said, picking up her bag from near the log and opening it to find the few mushrooms they had collected so far had been squashed in all the panic. The box with the key had only aided in their inevitable crushing. "We will be here longer than I had anticipated, though. Emma will now be working hard, I'm sure of it."

"Might have to start paying me," Emma teased as one of the dogs sniffed at her side before licking her bare arm.

"You owe me for nearly giving me a heart attack."

"I guess you make a good point," Emma said with a chuckle though her attention was firmly on the dog she was now petting.

"We will help, too," Nevan declared, jostling his bow over his shoulder.

"Yeah," Lord Walsh added, running a hand through his hair. "I'm not in the mood for hunting anymore."

"I wonder why," Sloane said beneath her breath.

Lord Walsh whistled, calling his other dogs to him, and then the group set off to search through the woods for mushrooms. Sloane felt on high alert as they did despite there being no longer anyone hunting.

Emma's joke had left her on edge.

"Your friend has an interesting sense of humour," Nevan said as he walked at her side.

"If you can call it that," Sloane replied, her gaze fixed on the ground as she continued her search. She just wanted to find the mushrooms and get out of the woods.

"It certainly got Connor's attention," he said, and Sloane looked up to see Emma had strolled away with Lord Walsh. Her friend was laughing as she walked with the lord, and Sloane found herself hoping that it wasn't too late for them.

"I think she already had his attention before this."

Nevan chuckled. "You're right about that, though pretending to be shot by an arrow may have been a bit extreme."

"She's hardly a desperate girl looking to catch the eye of a man." Sloane raised a brow. "If that's what you're expecting, you're going to be disappointed."

"I'm actually hoping that you're right." He smiled. "What about you? What impression should I have?"

Sloane dropped her gaze, resuming her search. "I don't think I am the person you should be asking about that."

"Why? Who would be a better judge of you than yourself?'"

"Anyone else," she said. She spotted a mushroom nestled in the crook of an exposed root and crouched to pick it.

"If you won't tell me, maybe you will spend more time with me so that I can make my own judgements." He knelt beside her, placing a finger beneath her chin and gently lifting it. Her heart raced at his touch and the way he looked deeply into her eyes. "I already know how beautiful you are, and from the brief time I have spent with you, I can see that you are a kind and brilliant woman. Now, I want to find more of what lies within."

She could feel a blush creeping into her cheeks.

"Come to tea tomorrow."

Sloane pursed her lips. "I work tomorrow."

"All day?" He asked, tilting his head to the side.

"Yeah," Sloane gave a small smile. "Yeah, unfortunately, I do."

"Then come for dinner," he said with a smile. "You don't work through dinner, do you?"

She shook her head. "I can come for dinner, but not tomorrow."

Nevan's smile grew as bright as the sun. "I'll have you whenever you let me."

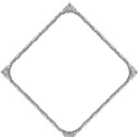

Sloane sighed while striding over to the counter to start unpacking her satchel. Very few mushrooms were within, but they would have to do until she collected more tomorrow. Having Nevan and Lord Walsh join her and Emma had proven to be more of a distraction than a help. Emma hadn't left Lord Walsh's side the entire time, so Sloane was keen to see her friend as soon as possible to find out what had happened between the two.

She could tell Emma had feelings for the lord. Hopefully, her running away hadn't deterred him from trying to pursue her.

Sloane bent and grabbed a bowl from beneath the bench to wash the mushrooms, along with a towel and some jars to store them. They would have been prepared in different ways; some fresh or pickled, whilst others would be dried out and ground into a powder depending on the species.

"You're back," Annabelle said as Sloane stood back up.

Sloane placed the items on the counter. "Yeah, just got in."

"You didn't collect much."

"We got distracted," Sloane replied with a sigh. "Emma pretended to get shot by an arrow—"

"That girl is going to get herself hurt for real one of these days with her theatrics."

The doorbell chimed, and in strode Rian with a basket in his hands.

"I didn't think we had any deliveries today," Annabelle said, approaching the man.

"You don't," he replied with a grin. "Just thought I'd check in."

"Well, aren't you the sweetest," Annabelle said, patting him on the arm and offering him a wide smile. Then, behind his back, where he couldn't notice her, she exaggeratedly pointed to him, mouthing 'key', and then shrugged.

Sloane was sure Nevan had been the one to send her the key, not that he had confirmed the gift was from him in the forest. Why Annabelle thought it was Rian was ridiculous. Rian was her friend.

Sloane felt her stomach twist. Maybe she was still feeling the effects of Emma's little stunt.

"I noticed you haven't added any supplies to your list for me," Rian said as he strode to stand opposite Sloane. "Do you have everything you need?"

"Mostly, for now," Sloane replied. "Just waiting on the candles."

"Ahh, yes," he grinned. "Otherwise, you can't wear clothes."

Sloane laughed, picking up the mushrooms and putting them onto the towel. "That's not what I meant, and you know it."

"Maybe," he chuckled. "But it is fun to tease you."

"Apparently," Sloane smirked. "Will you be going to the guard tournament?"

"Of course," he nodded. "Everyone attends."

"Some of us work." She picked up a mushroom, dusting it

off before placing it in the waiting jar.

"Yeah, but you won't be all day. I'm sure you can take a moment to come down like you do every year."

"How do you know I go every year?" she asked, looking up at him and raising a brow.

"I've seen you around."

"Stalker," she teased and subconsciously bit her lip.

"Sloane will go if her mystery man is there," Annabelle chimed in. "He'll probably bring you another gift and ask to escort you."

"Will he now?" Rian asked coyly. "And who is this man?"

"I have an idea," Sloane replied. "But don't ask because I'm not telling anyone who I think it is."

"I bet Emma knows," Annabelle pouted.

"Okay, anyone other than Emma."

Rian laughed. "I'm intrigued to see who she thinks it is."

"Welcome to the club," Annabella replied sarcastically. "We meet on Wednesdays."

"Don't you two have more interesting things happening in your lives than my love life?" Sloane asked with a pout.

"Nope," Rian said with a wink before departing from the store.

6

The sun was hotter than usual for the time of year as Sloane sat in the field, listening to her father recite her family's legacy.

"Couldn't we do this under the shade of a tree?" Sloane asked with a groan. Sweat beaded on her forehead, amongst other places, much to her dismay from sitting in the sun outside of town. She was glad her father was out of the house, but now even the golden key hung around her neck was beginning to feel warm between her breasts. She'd need to wash and change before returning to work; that was certain. "Maybe even in our garden at home?"

Her father shook his head. "This spot is significant." He pointed to the flat rock between them. It was fixed into the ground and had imagery carved into the flat surface. "Here is where our ancestors stood when they changed the world for the good."

"I still don't understand. If the Maker's history is so important, why is it such a secret?" she said, blowing out a breath. She was humouring him coming to the field today. She had a lot of work to do at the apothecary, yet he'd asked her here, and she couldn't turn down an opportunity to leave the house with him. He hadn't been anywhere in months.

"To protect them, Sloane," he replied with an exasperated sigh. "I've told you before; they can never know of the sacrifices we have made."

"*We* didn't do anything. The sacrifices were all in the past," she said. She pulled a blade of green grass from the ground and rolled it between her fingers. "Our ancestors supposedly paid the price, not us."

"And it is our duty to keep their sacrifice a secret for the continued safety of the world."

"I still don't understand how you can think we are the only ones who would possibly know about what happened to Valmenessia," she said. "It's a pretty big secret."

"The magic of a Maker was the strongest entity in existence," he said, removing his coat. She could see that he was also bothered by the heat thanks to the patches beneath his arms, even if he wasn't complaining about it like she was. "In creating the prison land, they had to remove the memories of what had happened. It was the only way to keep everyone safe and stop the whole world from being doomed."

"Sounds like a fairy tale."

"It sort of does," her father chuckled. "But it is serious. The tyrants had to be stopped. They believed they were gods and goddesses that walked the land. Their followers did terrible things in their names. If it weren't for our ancestors," he spread his arms wide. "All of this would be dust."

"So is this little gathering we have here," she began, opening her arms wide. "Meant to celebrate the day of their downfall?"

Her father had brought flowers with him, placing them near the stone plaque like he was paying respects to a grave.

"It is small, but it could not go unrecognised," he replied.

"Do these things keep the memories alive." He looked around them, awe filling his expression. "Here is where it all happened. Where the spell was cast, and our ancestors' sacrifice was made. Can't you feel it?"

"Not really."

"Close your eyes, Sloane," he said. "Let your body relax and just try to feel the magic."

Sloane did as she was told, steadying her breaths and trying as best she could to do as her father asked. She felt nothing except the heat from the sun. There was no magic. Yet she couldn't deny that she felt a little disappointed. Part of her wanted to believe what her father was saying—that maybe his studies were filled with facts rather than the beliefs of a man who was slowly losing his mind.

"Well?"

Sloane frowned, opening her eyes. "I'm sorry. I can't feel it."

"It will come," he said, rising to his feet. He held out a hand for her. "We will try again as much as we need to until you can feel your birthright."

"You're going to leave the house more often now? Does that mean you'll be coming back to work?"

"No," he shook his head. "My work now is our family history and helping you to connect with it."

"Does it bring in much coin?"

"Sloane..."

"What?" She snapped. "Your current venture won't feed us or pay our taxes. There is only so much I can do at the shop. After that, people will begin to ask questions and then what? I am not allowed to own the business. We will lose it all."

"This is much bigger than the apothecary. Than both of us."

"So I have to accept my fate? Eventually, we'll lose our income, and I will become a beggar?"

"Don't be so dramatic."

"You're the one being dramatic! Talking of magic and some family history of heroes."

"The Makers *were* heroes," her father sputtered, his cheeks reddening with anger. "They saved us all. Learning of their history, of *our* history, is the least we can do. Try not to behave like a spoilt brat. You won't become a beggar."

Sloane glared at her father. "No, I won't because someone is interested in me, and once I am married, I will be taken care of and won't need the apothecary or your crazy stories."

She jumped to her feet with her fist clenched at her sides.

"Do you love him?

"What?" Sloane asked, looking down at her father.

His eyes searched hers, a slight frown on his lips. "Do you love this man?"

"I—ah—I don't know yet," she replied, raising her chin. "But that's beside the point because I will be married one day."

Sloane turned, storming away from her father. She was so angry with him that he would put his need to learn about their family history, if it could even be called that, before her. He cared so much about their dead family, yet nothing for his blood who was still living.

Sloane was sorting newly made tonics the next day when another package arrived. She wasn't in the best mood after the night she'd had. Her father's night terrors had been awful. He'd yelled and screamed for hours and there had been nothing she could do to calm him. In the end, she'd sat on the opposite side of his bedroom, nestled under blankets on the floor and watched him until the two of them both fell asleep. She could have locked herself in her room and covered her ears with cushions to drown him out, but she'd have never forgiven herself if he had sleepwalked and gotten hurt.

Stifling a yawn with her elbow, she gave the delivery boy a coin, and he left her alone with the box in her hands. Her heart skipped in her chest at the prospect of what was inside, and her impatience dictated she immediately opened the box.

A simple sprig sat within. Sloane picked it up and, holding the twig between two fingers, inspected the white-green leaves. She recognised it instantly; she'd used the bark of the willow tree in some of her tonics for pain relief and knew it grew in only one place in Devotion.

"I hope that's not our only supply of willow," Annabella said as she approached. She placed a hand over her mouth and coughed. "The leaves won't help anyone."

Sloane shook her head. "It was another gift."

"Not as fancy as the key," Annabelle frowned and then gasped a moment later, startling Sloane. "They're clues! I love a good puzzle." She tapped her finger against her chin. "So first, you got a key, and what are keys for?"

"Opening things…"

"Yes, but what? Chests, doors—"

"Prison cells," Sloane said with a smirk.

Annabelle shot her a dirty look. "Your negativity isn't helping. I know you think you know who is sending you these gifts, but don't you want to know what they are trying to tell you?"

"There was a lot of knowing in that sentence," Sloane replied, then sighed. "Yeah, I guess you're right."

"Now, the willow. It's a tree, obviously," she said. "Used for tonics."

"And fertility," Sloane said, then frowned. She hoped Nevan wasn't planning to wed and bed her just to pop out some heirs hastily. He'd never mentioned children, not that they had known each other long enough to discuss much of what the future could hold.

"Oh, children!"

"I can barely take care of myself, let alone a child."

Sloane sighed; she hoped they were interpreting this gift wrong.

"Rebirth?" Annabelle posed. "Ooh! Maybe both combined, they are meant to be like opening the door to a new beginning. A romantic beginning."

"That actually makes sense and is way less frightening than the prospect of having a child right now," Sloane replied. "A new romantic beginning. A little cliché, but also really sweet."

"It is very sweet, indeed," Annabelle said, clasping her hands beneath her chin. She sniffed, and Sloane noticed the tip of her nose was tinted red.

"Though one day I would like to have children," Sloane admitted, placing the box on the counter. "The idea of having a family again is very tempting."

"You have a family."

"No, I don't," Sloane replied, walking over to the nearest shelves to tidy the display. "I have a mother who passed before I even got to meet her and a father who is more interested in his books than me. I want a family that is present. I need one."

Annabelle placed a hand on her shoulder, and Sloane sighed, turning to face the other woman.

"Until then, you have Emma and me," Annabelle said, pulling Sloane into a hug. "Oh, and Rian is always around." She laughed. "But you still have your father; he does love you. I know it."

"I wish he would show it," Sloane said, wrapping her arms around Annabelle. "Like he used to."

7

Dust floated in the air around her like the seeds of a dandelion after they had been wished upon. Sloane placed the back of her hand beneath her nose and sneezed. Cleaning and restocking the apothecary was a task she hated more than anything, and with Annabelle home sick for the day, it was going to take longer than usual.

The bell above the door chimed, and the sound made Sloane groan. *Couldn't people read anymore?*

"We're not open yet!" she called, not bothering to turn around.

"Even for me?" Rian asked, appearing at her side. He leaned against the shelf with his arms folded over his chest. The fabric of his grey shirt tightened around his biceps in the position.

"Depends on what you're here for," she replied with a smirk.

"I was thinking I might offer you a hand," he said. Then he stepped away, backing up towards the door. "But you look like you have it under control, so I'll leave you to it.

"Rian…" she groaned.

"Mmm?"

"If you could help," she said, putting on an exaggerated smile. "I'd be more than grateful."

He grinned broadly. "I guess I could stick around for a little."

Rian began helping by removing items from the shelves and placing them in boxes so Sloane could dust them. The two of them moved in comfortable silence, cleaning and tidying the entire wall of shelves in just over an hour, something that would have taken Sloane half the day on her own.

"Want a drink?" Sloane asked, dropping her cloth into one of the boxes and heading to the back room. "Water? Tea?"

"Water," Rian replied, picking up a vial from the small shelf on the counter. He held it up and chuckled. "Elixir for vigour and stamina."

Sloane rushed back into the shop front and snatched it from his hand with a laugh. "That's one of our best sellers."

"Really?"

"Yahuh," she grinned. "You'd be surprised what people buy."

"And to think, I thought your apothecary only catered to healing and hygiene," he replied, selecting another vial from the shelf. "What else do you have in here?"

Sloane made to grab the vial from his hand, but he wouldn't let it go. He laughed as she lunged, grabbing hold of the wrist of the hand holding the vial out of reach. But her attempt to retrieve the vial only led to her bumping into him, and as he took a step back to steady himself, Rian fell over the empty boxes taking her with him. She landed on his chest with an oof, her heart racing. Sloane groaned, lifting her head, and blew the tussled hair from her face.

"You're such a shit," she laughed, snatching the vial from his hand. "Why are you always teasing me?"

She looked at him, expecting a snarky remark in reply, but

instead found he was looking at her so intently. She was suddenly very aware of her body pressed to his, how his chest moved up and down beneath her with each breath, how his hand held her hip.

"Am I interrupting something?"

Sloane turned, eyes wide and mouth agape, to see Nevan standing in the middle of the apothecary with his hands behind his back and a slight smile on his face. His hair was styled impeccably, just like every other aspect of him. His clothing was pressed and of the latest fashion, gold buttons and expensive fabrics, making him look incredibly regal. She hadn't even heard the bell chime on the door.

"Ahh," Sloane said, snapping her mouth closed and scrambling off Rian. Her cheeks flushed as she stumbled, but Rian caught her, stopping her from falling on her ass and making even more of an embarrassment of herself. How must it have looked to find her lying on top of him? She hoped Nevan didn't read into it. She and Rian were friends. "No, we fell, that's all."

She smoothed down her purple skirt and smiled up at him. "Sorry about that."

"Nothing to apologise for," he replied with a little shake of his head. "Will you be working all day?"

Sloane nodded. "Annabelle is sick, so it is just me for the day."

He looked over her shoulder. "You don't work at the apothecary?"

"Just helping Sloane tidy up," Rian replied stiffly, coming to stand close by her side. She glanced at him; her brow raised at his tone. Rian was one of the friendliest people she knew; what had gotten into him?

"Rian is an old friend," Sloane said, slapping the back of her hand on his chest. "When he saw I was alone here, he offered to help. So, what brings you by?"

"I was walking down the street, thinking of you, and it looks like someone is watching over me because next thing I know, I spotted you through the window. An apothecary. It seems almost perfect that your family should run an apothecary. It's the closest thing humans have to magic … and you certainly seem to cast a spell on everyone around you," he replied, all charm.

He reached out, tucking a stray silver blonde hair behind her ear. She wasn't sure if it was his touch or what he said about the apothecary that warmed her. "I'm not sure if you are aware, but there is a guard tournament being held today," he added.

"I'm aware," she smiled, leaning into his touch. "That's why I'm here. With everyone out at Lord Walsh's property, it's the perfect time to tend to the apothecary uninterrupted."

The Lord's Guard Tournament was a tradition that occurred every harvest season. It was a competition for the guards to show off their skills to Lord Walsh and prove themselves worthy of protecting the city. Citizens were invited to watch, not only for entertainment but to serve as a warning of what they'd come up against if they chose to break the law.

"I heard the tournament is quite the spectacle for the neighbouring towns, not just Devotion itself. Seems a pity for you to miss it."

"Things need to be done, and Annabelle couldn't work today," she said. "Not to mention there will still be the occasional customer. The store is expected to be open. Speaking of which," she strode to the door, flipping the sign over. She turned back to Nevan. "I need to be here."

"Emma will be so disappointed. I convinced her to let me do the honour of escorting you. Can't your friend here help?" Nevan asked, angling his head to Rian. "He can stay and tend to the customers."

"Rian has already helped me today," Sloane said, looking between the two men. Neither had their eyes on her; both instead were having some sort of stare-off.

"If you need me," Rian said. "I will help." She opened her

mouth to reply but never got the chance. He turned, looking at her with the same intensity as before. "Whatever you need."

For some reason, his words felt like more than just an offer for assistance with cleaning the apothecary. Her heart skipped a beat, and she suddenly felt all too warm.

"It's settled then," Nevan said, and Sloane's attention was turned back to him. "I'll go collect my carriage and return in time for us to see the afternoon's events."

Sloane nodded, finding herself unable to speak. She watched Nevan depart, then turned to Rian and chewed her lip.

"If it's too much," Sloane began, fidgeting with her hands. "I can manage."

"Just say thank you," he replied. He smiled, but it didn't reach his eyes. The sight unsettled her.

"Thank you," she said, and he turned his back to her. His sudden coldness made her shiver.

"Lavender or rose?" the woman asked, holding the soaps in either hand towards her husband. He snapped out of his bored expression as she jiggled her hands beneath his nose and sniffed each. "Well?"

There had been no customers all morning; then, just as she was about to go upstairs to get cleaned up for Nevan's arrival, of course, her first customers of the day stepped through the door.

"Rose," the husband replied, and his wife smiled, seemingly happy with his answer.

"Wonderful choice," Sloane said, packaging the soap and sending them on their way.

She looked to help another customer who had been waiting

patiently only to startle. Rian stood beside her, chatting with a man about an elixir.

"Here," Rian chuckled, handing over the elixir and taking the man's money. "With this, it will no longer be an issue for you."

He winked, and the man grinned broadly before tipping his hat and striding away.

"What did you sell him?" Sloane asked, taking the coins from Rian.

"One of your stamina elixirs," Rian replied with a one-shouldered shrug. "You're right; they are popular. He had heard from a friend that takes it."

"See," she stuck out her tongue. "I told you."

He placed a hand over his heart. "I will never doubt you again."

"Learnt your lesson?"

"I have," he replied. He dropped her gaze, running a hand over the wooden top of the counter. "There's no one in the store. You should probably go get ready for lover boy."

"Don't call him that," she said, slapping him on the arm lightly. "I've only known him for a little while."

"He is very interested in you."

"You don't know that for sure."

He raised his brow at her.

"Okay fine," she sighed. "He is showing his intentions, but I'm so far below his status, and he's only here for a short time. He's probably just having fun while he's in Devotion and then will leave and forget all about me."

Rian grabbed her arm, drawing her close so that they were looking into each other's eyes. His voice was low as he spoke, sending heat into her lower belly. "There is no possibility that he could ever forget you, and that's if he was stupid enough to walk away from you in the first place. Fuck status; you are worth more than anyone because of what you have in here." He placed his hand gently over her heart, then moved to her temple, gently placing two fingers on her head. "And in here. Don't you ever think otherwise."

Sloane stared at him as he released her and stepped back, creating some distance between them that felt further than the physical steps he had taken. She felt like she should say something. But no words came to her because what could she possibly say in response to what he'd said?

"He's stepping out of his carriage," Rian said with a nod in the direction of the window.

She turned to see Nevan striding towards the door. He looked like a man who had the world at his feet.

"Shit," Sloane hissed, picking up her skirts and running upstairs. She passed her father, who was bent over a desk, examining something he had sprawled out before him. She didn't bother to stop and ask; she just quickly went to her room to change and fix her hair.

After deeming herself a little more presentable, she made her way back downstairs in a lavender dress with her hair loose and flowing down her back. She found both men standing in silence by the door. They both looked at her as she entered the store again.

"You look beautiful. Shall we?" Nevan asked, offering his hand.

Sloane nodded, taking his hand, and she spotted Rian shaking his head at the edge of her vision. She glanced at him, but he just smiled warmly at her.

"Thought I'd join you," Rian announced, turning the sign hanging on the door to read 'closed' to those on the street. "Nevan so kindly offered to give me a ride too."

"He did?" Sloane raised a brow.

Nevan gave a tight-lipped smile, his gaze intently on Rian. "I did."

"I can't leave the customers," Sloane sighed. She turned to

go back to the counter, only to have Rian wrap an arm around her waist and tug her back.

She didn't fight him. His action felt personal, more personal than when she'd found herself on top of him earlier that day. Unlike what had been an accident, now it was intentional ... comfortable even.

"They'll be fine," he replied, releasing her and nudging her towards the now-open door. "You close in a couple of hours anyway."

He gestured for her to exit first, and she ambled through the door to find Nevan's hand clasping tightly around hers as soon as she did.

"I guess," Sloane mumbled, not entirely convinced, as she let Nevan lead her to the carriage. She couldn't help but wonder what Rian was up to. Was this a game of his? Another way to tease her and make her squirm, maybe even annoy Nevan too?

8

The three climbed inside the carriage, Rian taking the spot opposite Sloane whilst Nevan sat at her side. She shot Rian a stern look, silently begging him to behave himself.

"Do other cities you've been to hold these sorts of tournaments?" Sloane asked Nevan, a smile on her face as they rode along the street.

"I have heard that some do. However, I've only been present for one other," he replied. "And I have a feeling today's will be quite different."

"Really? How?"

"Connor is a good lord, but he is young," Nevan said. The carriage wobbled along the road as they made their way out of the more densely populated area of Devotion. "Other cities have more experienced lords who use other methods. In the one I attended, the guards were made to fight civilians convicted of petty crimes who were given no weapons to defend themselves."

Sloane grimaced. "They wouldn't stand a chance."

"There was not one survivor," he said, patting her on the hand. "Though something can be said for harsh punishment as a deterrent for criminal behaviour."

"Devotion has very low crime," Rian stated, and Sloane looked up to see him staring impartially out the window. He may have been trying to appear bored, but she knew better. His finger was tapping away on his thigh. "The late Lord Walsh set a high standard, and I'm sure the new lord, though young as you've said, will do the same. He carries on traditions that his ancestors created. Mutual respect and a lord who cares for and provides for his people can go a long way to creating a city where citizens feel safe and happy."

Sloane opened her mouth but shut it quickly when Nevan spoke before she could. The tension was already rising in the carriage. If only she could get out and walk in the fields they travelled beside instead.

"I agree that Connor is a great man, but whether he does as his father had before him is yet to be seen. You are not privy to the inner workings of those with power, and that is no fault of your own, purely a side effect of your station," Nevan said, fixing Rian with a pointed look. "There is more to ruling than simply being happy or sad."

"It might surprise you to know that people in such lowly stations as *us*," Rian said, his sarcasm evident in his tone while his finger still tapped away. Sloane clenched her fist; she could have hit him. She silently begged him to shut up and just let it go. There was no need for an argument. "…can comprehend more than two basic emotions. The Lord is your friend, and you talk about him like—"

"Oh, look! Willow trees!" Sloane exclaimed almost desperately, taking matters into her own hands. If Rian wouldn't shut up, then she would shut him up for him. She looked out the window to the lord's estate up ahead and pointed to the trees.

"Don't they look beautiful?"

"My favourites are the White Willow that grow down by the lake," Rian said, his tone much softer than the one he had been using to speak with Nevan. "But these around Lord Walsh's property are also nice."

"A great scholar friend told me that the willow tree was an omen of pain and suffering," Nevan replied, and she turned her head to see him adjusting his coat.

Sloane scrunched her brow in confusion, but before she could get her thoughts together, the carriage pulled to a stop in front of Lord Walsh's estate. Nevan helped her from the carriage, and the trio walked along the path towards the tournament together.

Harvest Season was when the Walsh estate shone, especially in the daytime. The gardens were bright and colourful thanks to the blooming flowers, and the bushes were a vibrant green. Everything felt so alive. A feeling that seemed to bleed into the people gathered at the estate.

Many people from Devotion attended. Men were in their best suits and women in pretty dresses; some were even carrying parasols that they twirled over their shoulders. Children ran amongst the crowd, laughing and squealing with delight.

"What was that about?" Sloane scolded Rian, her voice low enough for only him to hear. People moved around them, but no one paid them any notice. Not even Nevan, who was busy speaking to his driver.

"Yeah, he was being a pompous ass, wasn't he?" Rian replied, looking over the heads of those crowded around them.

"You were purposely trying to start a fight," she hissed, her anger bubbling inside her.

Rian smirked as he finally looked at her. "So you agree he's an ass?"

Sloane growled, elbowing him in the ribs. "Why are you messing with me?"

"Come," Nevan said, appearing at her side. He took Sloane's

hand and dragged her away from her hushed argument with Rian. "Connor will have seats for us." He looked back to Rian, raising his voice over the crowd. "We might see you later."

Sloane looked behind her and stuck her tongue out at Rian before she was led away through the crowd to an enclosed area. She took a few breaths, trying to calm her frustration at Rian. She knew they liked to tease each other, but this was going too far.

Her mind drifted from Rian briefly when she spotted Melanie's husband and children. Despite being out in public, they didn't appear happy to be there. Sloane's heart ached for them. It had been a over a week and they were still no closer to finding out what happened to Melanie.

Sloane lost sight of them as Nevan pulled her along. The people around them began to thin, and she found herself standing before a doorman. Behind him, a floral arch surrounded by a fence signified an exclusive area. The man nodded in greeting, stepping out of the way for Nevan and Sloane to stride by.

"You're here!" Emma exclaimed, hurrying to Sloane's side as soon as she was inside. "I honestly didn't think you would come."

"I can be quite persuasive," Nevan said with a grin, stuffing his hands into his pockets.

"You've missed the first few rounds, but that doesn't matter," Emma said with a grin. "As you know, they save the best fighters for last."

Sloane glanced around as she followed Emma through the fenced-in area. It looked to be restricted to only those of the higher class in Devotion and had ample space for them to move about. A table laid with food stood at the centre for those who wished to leisurely dine in comfort as they watched the violent tournament take place. Despite the luxuries, it sort of felt like a pen for farm animals and beyond them were the free people, the wild animals. Sloane wasn't entirely sure what to make of that or which she saw herself as.

"Welcome, welcome," Lord Walsh said in greeting, his grey eyes bright as he shook Nevan's hand, and Sloane curtsied. "I'm glad you both are finally here. Emma has been eager to see you, Miss Maker."

"Thank you for having me here," Sloane replied. "I've only ever watched the tournament from the crowds."

Nevan leant down, whispering in her ear. "You won't have to endure that anymore. You belong here with us."

"The next round is starting," Lord Walsh declared, then moved to stand on a raised platform.

From up on the platform, he looked every bit the lord of the city. He was a tall man with a broad chest, but his comfortable demeanour made him feel smaller. Not in a minimising way, but more in a relatable one. Now, however, he felt almost regal. Lord Walsh raised a flag with his family crest upon it in the sky, and the crowd grew silent.

Anticipation filled the air as two guards strode onto the field in shining silver armour. One wore a white ribbon around his arm, the other black, distinguishing them from one another. They stood before the lord, who offered them good luck; then both moved to either end of the field. A low hum of chatter spread out as the crowd placed their bets on who would win—some for the fun of it and others for coin.

Lord Walsh dropped his hand, the flag fluttering, and the crowd erupted. At least, those outside the fenced-in area did. Around Sloane, the nobles returned to their conversations and food, clearly disinterested in the events on the field. She spotted Emma's mother laughing with some other women in the far corner while her friend's father stood nearby, deep in conversation with her brothers and some other men. None looked at the fighting guards, not even when the crowd beyond let out a cheer.

"They've never been interested," Emma said as if reading Sloane's thoughts. "This is just another opportunity for them to catch up on gossip and make connections with other important people." She said the last part in a low voice that she often used to mimic her father, earning a chuckle from Sloane. "You can see why I snuck out to be with you out there all the time."

"With us lowly people."

"You know I don't see you that way." Emma squeezed Sloane's wrist. "Connor is watching. That's the most important thing."

"I guess you're right," Sloane replied, bumping her side into Emma playfully.

"I always hated coming into this area with my family," Emma said, looking around with a frown on her face. "I never felt like I fit, but having you and Connor here makes all the difference. Everything is perfect right now, don't you think?"

It should have been. If it weren't for the sinking feeling in Sloane's gut, that is.

They watched a few rounds before Sloane found herself being pulled away from the tournament by Nevan. He held her hand gently, leading her outside of the fenced-in area along a shrub-lined path. A few people were taking a stroll around the Manor's gardens as the afternoon sun slowly made its descent.

"I know you were enjoying yourself," Nevan said with a charming smile. "But I couldn't resist sweeping you away so I could have you all to myself."

Sloane blushed, averting her gaze and biting her lip to hold back her own smile.

"Tell me about you," Nevan said. He squeezed her hand, tugging her closer to his side. "I want to know more."

"Anything in particular?" she asked, her heart quickening in her chest at their closeness.

"Your hopes and dreams."

"Nothing big then," Sloane replied with a small shaky laugh.

She thought about it for a moment. What did she want? Sloane had had many dreams over the years. To one day take over her father's business, to be married and have children, to visit Valmenessia and learn magic, learn to paint, dance at as many balls as she could, see an Elementum magic show, taste every flavour of cake available ... There was one thing all those dreams had in common.

"I just want to be happy," she said finally.

Nevan looked at her, a brow raised. "Are you happy?"

Sloane felt suddenly deflated. The question, though simple, felt deeper than she had thought it would. "I guess."

"Don't I make you happy?" he asked, pulling her to a stop.

"You do," she said, stepping closer to him and placing a hand flat on his chest. She didn't want him to feel bad. It wasn't his fault she was unsure of herself at the moment. "Of course."

"But there *is* something making you unhappy." He looked down at her, his eyes searching hers for answers.

"We don't have to talk about it," she said, stepping back and walking along the path once more. She looked back when she didn't hear him follow. "We are having a nice afternoon."

"I never see your family around," he said. He stuffed his hands into his pockets and strode towards her. "Your parents?"

"I never knew my mother. She passed when I was born," Sloane replied. "My father isn't overly social anymore."

"Siblings?"

"Nope, just me."

"Has your family always been in the apothecary business?"

"Yeah," she replied without elaborating. She didn't want to talk about her ancestors or how they had all been involved in similar occupations. It made her think too much of her father's obsession. She lived through it every day, so talking about it in moments when she was afforded a reprieve was not ideal. Bringing up her ancestors now when she felt Nevan's questions were unintentionally deep was even worse. "My family is boring. Let's talk about you."

"I have three older brothers, my parents are still alive, and all of my relatives are busy climbing social ladders. They don't approve of me wasting my education to travel around the place," he said as if rattling off a rehearsed list. "They have a view of how life should be, and I see it differently. They want social power. I want another kind."

"Another kind?" Sloane scrunched her brow.

He laughed. "Nothing sinister. I just want something different to what I was brought up to believe I could have."

Sloane chewed her lip, unsure of what he was saying. What other power was there for humans other than what society gave them?

They'd made their way around the garden, steering back towards the tournament, when Sloane spotted Rian in the crowd. He was smiling, talking with a small group. A woman she recognised as a customer looked up at him all doe-eyed, and a twinge rippled through Sloane's gut.

The woman had come in the previous day for a cream for some rash on her skin. It was probably contagious, and being that close to Rian would risk him catching it. Sloane frowned; the woman was being careless. Yep, that's what was irritating Sloane.

"Something wrong?" Nevan asked, and she realised she was still frowning.

"That woman is going to get Rian sick," she said, taking a step forward, only to have a restraining hand on her arm stop her.

"Sloane," Nevan said in a tone she didn't like, as if he was speaking to a child or pet. "He can take care of himself."

"I'd usually agree, but he doesn't have all the facts."

"It's not your place to tell him."

"He's my friend," she insisted.

"Yes, but he is with his other friends, and maybe that woman is more. If he is courting her, then whatever it is, it's between them and has nothing to do with you."

Sloane sighed heavily. "Fine."

"Come on," he said, drawing her away. "Emma and Connor are most likely wondering where we are by now."

Sloane continued to frown, glancing back occasionally at Rian and the rash woman as Nevan led her away. As much as she hated to admit it, Nevan was right. The two looked to be close. If Rian was courting the woman, then it was none of her business. He hadn't mentioned anything to her, but that didn't mean it wasn't true. There were possibly a lot of things he didn't say. She kept secrets from him, too, after all. It was possible she might not know him as well as she thought she did.

Sloane's stomach sank. She didn't like the thought of that at all.

REBECCA CAMM

9

Sloane awoke to find her father standing in the doorway of her bedroom. Sunlight flooded in from the open door, illuminating the small space she called her own. As they lived above the apothecary, their home was modest in that they had a bedroom each and a living area for sitting and eating. Though, at the moment, the living space was filled with her father's obsession so it was more of a large study that she ate in.

Her room, however, was untouched by her father's interests. In here, she had her books on various remedies, sketches she'd done of various plants, and treasures she'd collected from her walks, such as interesting rocks or flowers she'd dried out. Her cupboards contained her clothing. It was mostly simple items that suited her profession, though there were a few dresses she'd purchased for dances and, of course, her mother's dress. The room was as yet untouched by her father and was her little piece of the world all for herself.

"Is everything alright?" Sloane asked, pushing herself up into a sitting position in her bed and fussing with the blankets. She rubbed her eyes and frowned at her father.

"This letter came for you," he replied, stepping closer. He held it out, and she took it eagerly. Anticipation sparked in her at the prospect of another clue to add to the key and the willow. Or perhaps more, an explanation or revelation…

She opened the envelope, breaking the red wax seal, and took out the letter inside. She began unfolding it, eager to read what had been written, only to pause, remembering her father's presence. She glanced up, noting how he watched her keenly.

"Is there something else?"

He shook his head. His features were drawn, sadness filling his gaze. "I'll leave you to it." He turned, shuffling towards the door. He paused at the threshold, running a hand through his blond hair. "Sloane…"

"You'll need to get used to it," she said before he could finish his sentence. "If it isn't this man, then another will court me. I don't want to be alone like you."

The words came out harsher than she intended, but they needed to be said. He needed to understand that she had a life to live, and she wasn't going to let it slip from her fingers. Her conversation with Nevan had her reflecting on her life. She wanted to be happy, and following her heart was going to make that single dream come true.

"I hope with all my heart for the same," her father replied. Then he left her to the letter with his shoulders slumped.

She finished unfolding the paper. Her excitement quickly turned to confusion as she found only a single word.

Hawkins.

Flipping the paper over, she found nothing else on the other side. Sloane frowned; what could Hawkins mean? She hadn't heard it before, at least, she hadn't thought she had. Was it a name? A place? Maybe she'd have to ask Emma or Annabelle when she saw them next.

A key, a spring of willow and now, Hawkins.

Sloane flopped back onto her pillows, pressing the letter to her chest as she looked up at the ceiling. What did all these clues mean? What was Nevan trying to tell her?

Rian had not been in to make any deliveries, which was odd because she was sure he would bring the candle order or at least pop in as usual just to say hi. She kept wondering whether he was mad at her, but she'd done nothing to warrant him being so. He hadn't gotten along with Nevan. That much was clear. Though, it had nothing to do with her.

She chewed her lip.

His and Nevan's interactions didn't have anything to do with her, did they? She shook her head. No, they didn't. They were grown men, and it was not her place to get between them. Not to mention, Rian knew that Nevan was interested in her, and if he was truly her friend, he wouldn't have made things so awkward. Plus, there was that woman who looked all cosy next to him at the tournament. Maybe he'd caught her rash?

The bell on the door chimed, and in strode Nevan with one hand in his coat pocket and a smile that tugged up at one side of his face.

"How do you feel about dinner?" he asked, stopping before her.

"The event or the meal?"

The door opened again, and Emma and Lord Walsh entered,

the former laughing at something the lord had said. Outside, several guards were stationed around the lord's carriage, disrupting the flow of townsfolk moving about the street.

"Both."

"Positive," Sloane grinned.

"Good," Nevan replied, reaching for her hand. He lifted it to his lips, kissing her knuckles. "Because I am officially inviting you to dine with me."

"With us," Lord Walsh said, leaning his hip on the counter. Nevan's composure dropped, as well as his hold on her hand, his gaze narrowing on the lord, but he was quick to fix his features. "Emma and I will be there too."

"I might be busy," Emma called from where she was examining products on a shelf. "I have a very busy schedule."

"Cancel your plans," Lord Walsh replied, pushing off the counter and going to her. "We are having dinner with our friends."

"I don't know if my father and mother will approve," she said, pursing her lips though the action did nothing to hide her smile or the teasing in her eyes.

"I'll go speak to them now," he declared, striding towards the door, and Emma laughed, rushing after him.

The door chimed once again as they left, and the store was suddenly all too quiet.

"You'll come?" Nevan asked hopefully.

Sloane nodded. "Yes."

"I look forward to it," he leaned forward over the counter, and Sloane felt as though she were being pulled towards him. She pushed up on her toes, her heart fluttering at the prospect of a kiss from Nevan, only for a sneeze to scare the shit out of her. She jumped back, looking down to where Annabelle sat on the floor, her back leaning up against the counter.

"You scared me!" Sloane scolded.

"Not my fault you forgot I was here," Annabelle replied, wiping her nose with a handkerchief. "Though your visitors have been quite entertaining from what I can hear, so I don't blame you."

Nevan backed up, a smile on his face. "Next time," he said, a promise rather than a question. "I'll see you at dinner."

"See you then," she called as he left the store.

The instant he was out of view, Sloane turned on Annabelle, her hands on her hips.

"He was going to kiss me."

"I'm sorry," Annabelle sighed, stuffing her handkerchief into her pocket. "I tried to stay quiet; I really did."

Sloane's anger deflated instantly at Annabelle's sincere expression. "Did you find the wax, at least?"

Annabelle rose to her feet, lifting a bag as she went and deposited it on the counter. "Yes, so we can now seal the vials, but maybe we should save some and try to mould them into candles. I thought Rian would have made the delivery by now."

"Me too," Sloane grumbled, then stood up taller, holding her chin high. "And I'm going to find out where he is."

She stormed from the apothecary and out onto the street. Nevan, Emma and Lord Walsh were long gone, the carriage and guards along with them. Sloane marched down the street. She knew Rian's customers, so it was only a matter of following his usual route to find him. If she had to go to each stop, then so be it. Sloane was a woman on a mission as she strode through the streets of Devotion. The first two locations showed no sign of Rian, but the owners said he had been by. Knowing that only made her more annoyed that he had skipped her shop.

Her frustration grew with each place she visited, and by the time she spotted his wagon outside McArcher's pub, she was furious.

After giving his horse some quick pats, because he was a good boy and shouldn't pay for his owner's bad behaviour, Sloane stormed into the pub. She spotted Rian standing at the bar, a mug in hand, as he spoke with a server. Though when the man behind the bar saw Sloane, he angled his head towards her before scooting away from Rian to serve other customers.

Rian gave her a quick look, grimaced, and then returned to his drink.

Asshole.

She marched through the tiny pub and grabbed his arm, forcing him to face her.

"Hey," Rian said, shrugging out of her grip.

"Hey yourself," she snapped. "Where have you been? You never came by the apothecary."

"I've been busy."

"Drinking? Funny how you made time for your other deliveries but not mine."

"I don't have any deliveries for you."

"Oh yeah?"

"Yup," he replied, taking a swig of his beer.

Sloane narrowed her gaze at him, then spun around, storming from the pub. Outside, she climbed into his wagon and searched through the undelivered boxes, being far from careful as she shoved things out of the way.

"What do you think you're doing?" Rian growled, hopping up onto the wagon after following her outside.

Sloane smiled broadly, spotting exactly what she'd been looking for. "Finding my delivery." She stood tall, pointing at the box of candles. "I thought you didn't have my delivery. I'd wager these other few boxes are the rest of them."

"They might be for someone else," he said, folding his arms over his broad chest.

Sloane set her features. "They're not."

"Fuck, Sloane." He threw his hands into the air. "Fine, they're yours, but I was going to deliver them first thing tomorrow morning."

"Why not today?"

"Because I needed not to see you today, okay?" He turned

his back to her, climbing down from the wagon.

Sloane felt as though he'd slapped her, but that didn't stop her from following him. He wasn't going to get away that easily. "What? Why?"

"I have my reasons, and I don't have to tell them to you," he replied, running a hand through his hair. "The whole world doesn't revolve around you."

"I never said it did," she snapped, almost running into his chest as he stopped and turned abruptly. "But I would like to know why *my* friend doesn't want to see me."

"That's exactly it," he shook his head.

"What?" She backed up a step, her hands on her hips.

"Nothing," he grumbled. "Don't you have somewhere to be? Someone rich and powerful you can hang around?"

"Excuse me?" Sloane poked her finger into his chest and glared. "What's that supposed to mean?"

"You're attracted to coin and social status," he replied, his words cutting her. He shoved her finger away. "I never thought you were like that, and yet you've jumped at the first wealthy person in sight."

"I didn't jump at anyone!"

"No, of course not," he rolled his eyes. "You just so happen to be friends with a lawmaker's daughter, the lord of the city, and are now being courted by the recently arrived man with more coins than he could ever know what to do with."

"I've been friends with Emma since I was a child!" Sloane shouted at him. Around them, people were stopping to watch their fight, but she didn't care. Who did Rian think he was, accusing her of only being friends with people who had wealth or status? "And the others are by pure chance! I don't go seeking people out based on what advantages they could give me!"

"Could have fooled me." He turned his back to her again and stalked towards the pub. "Run along, Sloane. I'm sure there's some exclusive tea you should be attending with your fancy friends."

She didn't move, her whole body frozen with rage as she stared after him. A single tear burned down her cheek, that she quickly wiped it away. Rian was wrong about her, she knew that, but his words had stung, nevertheless.

10

Emma's carriage arrived at sunset. Sloane had been in a bad mood all afternoon since her run-in with Rian. She didn't understand why he'd behaved as he had today—the way he'd spoken to her. She kept telling herself not to let his attitude ruin her entire day, but she found herself unable to shake her feelings and the effect it was having on her.

Stepping into the carriage that would take her to dinner, Sloane was relieved to see that her best friend looked like she was about to burst at the seams with something to say. As soon as they started to move, words spilled from her lips faster than the horses pulling them along.

"I think Connor, I mean Lord Walsh, is going to propose," Emma blurted, just as unable to hold in her smile as her words. "He came to speak to my parents with his mother yesterday. I wasn't allowed to be in the room, but why else would they come?"

"That's amazing!" Sloane replied, genuinely happy to see

her friend smiling as she was. "I know you weren't keen on an arranged marriage, but it looks like your father chose well."

"He did. Can you believe it?" Emma said, her voice hitching high at the end. "If you'd asked me a month ago whether I thought the man who sired me would be able to choose someone who I'd be happy to spend my life with, I would have laughed in your face. Yet here we are." Emma sighed, reaching for Sloane's hands. "And think about it, this time next year we might both be married."

"Maybe," Sloane replied, drawing out the word as she sat back in her seat.

"I thought things were going well between you and Nevan?" Emma's happiness from a second ago vanished, making Sloane feel like a bad friend.

"They are. Everything is fine. He's wonderful and caring, and let's not talk about me," Sloane said, trying to get back the excitement and happiness. "You might be getting engaged! I want to know more details about that."

Emma chuckled. "Nice try. Tell me what's wrong."

Sloane didn't open her mouth. She didn't want to ruin Emma's announcement any more than she already had.

"Spill," Emma commanded, bumping her side with Sloane's.

"Fine! It has nothing to do with him, though," Sloane said, crossing her arms over her chest. "I had an argument with Rian today, and I have no idea why. Okay? Let's not talk about it."

"Maybe he's jealous," Emma suggested with a smirk. "I mean, who wouldn't be? You're stunning and smart and all-around amazing."

Sloane rolled her eyes, though she couldn't help a smile on her face at her friend's words. "You might see me like that, but Rian doesn't."

"Are you sure?" Emma teased. "He's always at the apothecary, even when he's not making deliveries. And you two have this whole easy banter thing."

"We do not."

"You do," she said with a wink. "Don't deny it."

"Whatever," Sloane said. "It doesn't matter because we are on our way to dinner with two men who don't confuse my brain, and I don't want to think about Rian."

"Sure you don't," Emma whispered under her breath.

Sloane groaned, sagging in her seat and earning a laugh from her friend.

They pulled up to Lord Walsh's manor, candles bordering the stone steps and lighting a guided path to the front door. Servants approached the carriage to help them out by the hand, and the two women made their way inside to find Lord Walsh and Nevan waiting in the hallway.

"Lord Walsh," Sloane said, dipping into a curtsey.

"Don't bother with that," Lord Walsh said with a wide smile. "We're friends now."

She rose with a slight blush on her cheeks. Friends with the lord of Devotion. It had been pure chance for her to become friends with Emma; the woman moved in circles well above her own, but now the lord too?

"Hello," Nevan whispered as he took her hand, then stepped back to allow his gaze to run over her. "You look beautiful."

Her blush deepened. She had chosen her best dress for the evening, an A-line dress made of lavender-dyed fabric that flowed to her feet. The sleeves were short, and a cape was attached to her shoulders, creating a train behind her. It had been her mother's dress, one of the few things her father had held onto over the years. The golden key hung around her neck, hidden beneath the fabric of her bodice.

The dinner wasn't anything special to warrant her wearing it; however, after she'd argued with Rian, she had chosen it to help bolster her mood, just as with her other attempts to distance the argument from her thoughts, it hadn't worked, though.

"Thank you," she replied, quickly glancing at his attire.

Tonight he was in all black; his shirt, trousers and coat blending into one another, except for his snake pin. It was the same colour, yet it stood out like a beacon against the rest of his clothing. "You scrub up pretty nicely yourself."

"Scrub up?" Nevan chuckled.

"You haven't heard that before?"

He shook his head. "Some of the things you say are cute."

Sloane smiled though it was hard not to feel patronised by his comment. *Cute? Like a child?*

They followed Lord Walsh into the dining room to find the place decorated exquisitely. Sloane couldn't help but wonder whether it had been set up for dinner or if it was always like this. Candles burned brightly in sconces around the room and in the candelabras that sat on the table. In their glow, the table was set up with glossy patterned plates and silverware with intricate detailing.

As Sloane sat beside Nevan, Rian's words crept into her mind. She shoved them down swiftly. He was wrong. She was not enticed by money and power.

Lord Walsh and Nevan fell into conversation as the food was promptly served. Staff with impeccable posture walked on silent feet, appearing at her side to deposit roast vegetables and meats onto her plate. Sloane didn't know what to make of it. She'd never been served like this in her life, and it felt odd for someone to decide not only her portions but what she would be eating too. She noticed that Emma's and her plates were given considerably smaller amounts of certain dishes than the men's.

Emma smiled at her from across the table, seemingly having noticed Sloane's discomfort. Her friend looked completely at home, yet Sloane couldn't feel any more out of place.

"Sloane," Lord Walsh said, setting his knife and fork beside his plate. "Your father's apothecary is quite the business. Everyone I know purchases their remedies from his store. He should be proud of his skills not only in producing tonics and the like but in business too."

"Thank you," Sloane said, her smile not quite reaching her eyes.

"Sloane does a lot at the apothecary," Emma said as the servants collected their dirty plates.

"Yes, making sure the store is presentable for customers is very important, too," Nevan said, his hand dropping to her thigh and squeezing.

"She does more than that," Emma replied, only to receive a chuckle from Nevan.

Sloane didn't react. She wasn't really listening to the conversation anymore or paying attention to the servants around her.

Dinner felt wrong.

Everything felt wrong.

Suddenly, she felt all too warm and her dress too tight. She stood abruptly, surprising the others and almost knocking over the dessert in front of her.

"Sorry," she said, dropping her napkin on her chair. "I need some air."

She quickly strode from the room, eager to escape. She could hear Emma and Nevan talking behind her, but she didn't bother to listen to what they were saying. Their voices were muffled anyway, so there wouldn't have been any point. Instead, Sloane continued out in the hallway, unsure where she was going, just that she couldn't be in the dining room any longer. Her breathing was becoming ragged, and she clutched her chest, the hallway tilting of its own accord despite the fact she was sure she was walking perfectly fine.

"Sloane," Nevan called, his footsteps pounding on the floor. He was evidently running to catch up.

She slowed, though not to let him reach her, more so that she didn't tumble as her vision clouded. She pressed her hand against the wall and shut her eyes, bracing herself.

"Everything alright?" Nevan asked. He put his hand on her shoulder.

How could she answer that when she didn't know? "I'll be fine," she replied, breathing deeply, her hand pressed to her stomach. Her words hadn't been a lie because she would be fine, maybe not right now, but she was sure that she'd be fine at some point in her future. Counting slowly, she regained her composure, or at least as much of it as she could and turned to face him.

He pressed his lips to hers. At first, it had startled her. She wasn't expecting him to kiss her, especially as she had just been in a panic. But then she welcomed it, hoping the kiss would fix her current emotional state.

Unfortunately, it didn't.

It felt so wrong, just like everything else did.

Sloane stepped back, fidgeting with her hands. "What does Hawkins mean?"

"Excuse me?" Nevan's features scrunched. "Is it a person?"

"And the key?"

"What key?" he replied, reaching for her, but she moved before he could grasp her. "Sloane, you are making no sense. I shouldn't have kissed you; you weren't in the right state. I just thought you looked so beautiful and lost. I was wrong. We should find somewhere for you to lie down."

"Is everything okay?" Emma asked, walking towards them.

"She needs to rest," Nevan said, trying to get hold of Sloane once more, but she wouldn't let him. He gave up, his hand dropping to the side as he and Emma fell into conversation about Sloane's wellbeing.

Sloane's mind ran over all the gifts she'd been given. Nevan hadn't sent a single one. He hadn't sent them, but someone had.

Her panic twisted into anger, her fists clenching at her sides.

"I should take you home," Emma said, placing a hand on Sloane's back.

"No." She stepped away from Emma. "I've got something

I need to do."

Emma's brows rose. "I don't think—"

Sloane picked up her skirt and ran down the hallway. "I'll tell you later! I promise!"

11

Sloane ran from the dinner, not caring who saw her. Her mind was fixed on one thing alone.

Rian had been sending her the gifts. She was sure of it.

Holding her skirts as she raced down the front steps of the mansion, her slippers hit the gravel path just as thunder rumbled overhead and the clouds released a torrent of rain. Heavy droplets fell, matching her mood.

Her heart pounded in her chest like the beat of a warm drum. How dare Rian send her those gifts to confuse her? He wasn't shy about teasing her, but this was a new low. She couldn't believe he had sent her random objects to mess with her head and make her second guess herself.

Heading down the drive, her skirts became heavy and slowed her pace, much to her frustration. She fumbled with the weight, cursing her dress. It would take her hours to reach Rian in this state.

Deciding she had already thrown away all sense of decorum,

Sloane hurried towards the nearest carriage with no driver. Whomever it was must have gone to seek shelter from the rain, and, unfortunately for him, she was going to take advantage of that. Freeing the horse, she beckoned it away from the carriage and attempted to climb on, only to find her dress far too heavy.

With an exasperated sigh, she pulled at the ties on her back, releasing the fabric. The dress fell to the muddy ground before she quickly gathered it up. Silently apologising to her mother, Sloane draped it over the horse's back, and with only her cotton slip to cover her, she climbed onto the horse.

"Please," she said to the horse through the rain as she urged it forward. "Don't you let me down, too."

The animal took off into the stormy night. Luck was finally on her side. The horse raced down the drive and onto the dirt road that was now a muddy mess. She held on tight, desperate to see Rian and confront him. He would know just how angry she was when she was done.

Sloane had thought they were friends, that the bickering had been a fun game. She thought back on the gifts that made no sense, of the way he had been when Nevan was around. The eye rolls and arguments, all the ways he made her second guess what was happening between Nevan and her. And then the argument today, the final move in the game he was playing. Rian had taken it too far.

As she neared his home, the rain eased. The droplets were now becoming gentle touches against her skin. She should have been shivering, but she was too angry to feel anything beyond the thrill within her. Out the front of his home sat his delivery wagon. She led the horse to the shelter adjoined to Rian's home and dismounted, tying it up beside Hawk. Rian's horse gave the newcomer barely a glance before returning to chewing on hay.

Hawk.

Hawkins.

Fuck, how did she not see that? Her anger grew. He had

her puzzling over his horse's name. Sloane stomped her foot, startling the horse who'd brought her there.

"Shit, sorry," she said, reaching out to calmly stroke the stead's head, then moved to give Hawk a couple of pats too. It wasn't his fault his owner was an asshole.

Turning to the shelter's entrance, she came face to face with Rian. He stood at the doorway that connected the shelter and his home, with the warm glow of a fire illuminating him from behind.

"What are you doing here?" he asked, his voice thick. She shivered despite not being able to see his eyes which she felt so intensely on her. She could only imagine how much of her he saw as she stood there in her drenched slip. "Annabelle said you were having dinner with…" His voice trailed off, his shoulders slumping.

"What is your problem?" she hissed, marching towards him. "I was trying to be happy, and you just had to play your little games, didn't you?"

"What games?"

"This!" she reached for the golden chain around her neck, holding up the key. "The willow! Oh, and Hawkins, nice work using your horse's name! You sent all this to me. Why?"

"I was trying—"

"I know we like to tease each other, but this is a new low for you." She folded her arms over her chest, ignoring how wet her slip was and how her naked body was most definitely visible beneath despite the lack of light. "Going out of your way to ruin whatever relationship I could have had with Nevan by sending this stuff to confuse me. I thought *he* sent them to me. I looked so foolish when he had no idea what I was talking about. Not to mention your terrible attitude whenever he was around. Were you trying to sabotage me?"

"Sloane—"

She shivered, from the cold or the way he said her name,

she wasn't sure. "Why don't you want me to find someone? Why play this trick on me?"

"It's not a trick," he said forcefully, bridging the gap between them so that she now had to look up to see his face. His hands landed on her upper arms, holding her in place. "I sent you those things because I'm too much of a coward to tell you how I feel. I thought if I told you outright, you'd think I was messing with you." He breathed out an exasperated sigh, and his hands tightened on her arms. "Which happened anyway."

"I don't understand," she shook her head. "We—you've never been interested in me like that."

A smile tugged at his lips. "I visit you every day, Sloane."

"You make deliveries," she said softly, the lie in her words clear by the time she'd finished her sentence. He didn't always make deliveries, yet he was there each day for a chat, a chance to tease Annabelle or to help with something. She shook her head. "Rian—"

"I love when you say my name," he said. "Even when you're shouting it at me because you're pissed at something I've done."

"Why did you wait until someone else had shown interest in me?" she asked, her anger fizzling.

"I didn't," he said with a huff. "That jerk rocking up was pure coincidence. And by the way, that terrible attitude you mentioned, wasn't it obvious I was jealous of him? Because I am. Plain and simple."

"You were jealous?"

"He has your attention," he replied. "And not only that, he was able to tell you how he felt outright."

"I would have believed you. If you told me."

"Sure you would have," he chuckled.

She looked into his eyes, searching for any sign of his teasing. But came up short. This wasn't a game.

Sloane had resigned herself to the thought that they would only ever be friends, that he wasn't interested in her in a romantic way. She'd long put that idea to bed.

Thinking back now on his presence every single day in her life. The way he was always there for her, helping her and putting her first, bringing a smile to her face. She couldn't believe she'd been so blind for so long. The man had been right under her nose, and she'd failed to see him.

"I believe you now," she said, wrapping her arms around his neck and pulling him down towards her. Their lips met, and Rian didn't hesitate to hold her closer to him, his hands moving to grip firmly over her hips. She melted against him as their mouths moved, and a hunger deep inside her grew. *This*. This felt right.

Rian scooped her up, her legs hooking around his middle, and he carried her inside, his mouth never leaving hers. Sloane ran her hands through his hair, then let her exploring take her down his neck to where she gripped his shoulders.

Thunder rumbled, and the rain began to pour once more outside, but it was nothing compared to the storm that was growing in Rian's small home. Sloane yelped as he dropped her onto the bed, and he grinned down at her, his heated stare running over her body.

"That thing doesn't leave much to the imagination," he said, reaching down to lift the skirt.

Sloane slapped his hand away and bit her lip. "I was wearing a dress earlier, though it wasn't practical to ride in."

He slowly knelt at the foot of the bed, his hands slipping under her skirts to run up her thighs. "I'm not complaining."

She shivered against his touch, despite the heat growing between her legs. She'd never done anything like this before with anyone. Suddenly she felt self-conscious, nerves fluttering in her stomach, and she stilled.

"Are you okay?" he asked, looking up at her. "We can stop."

She shook her head. "No, I want to be with you. It's just…" She looked up at the ceiling. "You're my first."

The bed dipped, and Rian appeared in her line of sight, his

body hovering just above hers. He looked down at her, his face filled with so much tenderness that her heart squeezed in her chest. She couldn't believe that she'd thought there would be anyone else than him.

He was all she wanted.

"We'll take it slow, and you can tell me to stop at any time."

Sloane nodded, lifting her lips to his. The kiss was slow this time, filled with passion rather than lust. He lowered himself over her, her legs parting so that he could rest between them. She felt his hardness push up against her through his trousers, accompanied by a need deep inside her. Rian's fingers ran along her chest, and then he tugged down the thin strap of her cotton slip, uncovering her breast.

His face dropped, and he drew in her nipple, eliciting a gasp to escape her. His hand continued to venture downwards before slipping beneath her slip. She sucked in a breath as his fingers caressed her, her body arching into his touch.

She reached for the buttons of Rian's shirt and ran her fingers down them, unbuttoning each one until she could press her hands to his exposed firm chest. His heart beat rapidly within, and his skin was as hot as she imagined hers was as well. She pushed his shirt over his shoulders and instantly felt the loss of his hands against her skin as he reared back to remove it completely.

"You're perfect," he said, looking down at her.

He gripped the edge of her slip, drawing it up, and she lifted her body to let the damp fabric slide up her skin until he'd removed it completely. Yet, even though it hadn't hidden her very well, she suddenly felt very exposed before him.

"Utterly devastatingly beautiful." Rian's voice was husky as he gently ran the back of his hand over her. Starting at the centre of her chest and slowly caressing downwards until he was rubbing her between the legs once more.

Sloane felt as though her body were being wound tight, a need building in her, and when he pushed his fingers inside, that need only grew. She was panting, aware of every sensation against her skin or lack thereof. She pulled him towards her, his chest pressing to hers as his lips moved against her mouth. His tongue swept along the seam of her lips, and she opened for him, wanting more.

Pleasure built, faster and faster, and then she arched her back and cried out his name. Her body shuddered with the most overwhelming feeling she'd ever experienced. Rian's fingers continued to move inside her, drawing out her pleasure until she felt her whole body soften into the bed.

Rian ran kisses along her collarbone and up her neck towards her lips, where he captured them once more.

He had given her so much pleasure, and yet, she wanted more. She could feel his hardness straining in his trousers against her thigh, and she reached down to unbutton and free him. Rian groaned at her touch as she ran her hand along his length.

"I want to feel you inside me," she breathed.

He kissed her. "How could I possibly deny you anything right now?"

His hand encircled her wrist, drawing it up above her head, then repeated the same with her other. He held onto her as his knees spread her legs apart, and he slowly pushed inside her.

"Is this what you want?" he asked, moving without urgency, letting her adjust to him.

"Yes," she panted, wrapping her legs around him and forcing him to close the distance. She gasped, a mix of pleasure and pain rushing through her.

This is exactly what she wanted, for him to be as close to her as he possibly could. She felt like she needed to touch every inch of him. Nothing would ever be enough when it came to satiating how much she wanted him.

Needed him.

Rian moved his hips, and his pace quickened. He looked deep into her eyes as her pleasure once more rose to an almost unbearable point. Her body arched, anticipating her release.

"I love you," he whispered.

With those words, she came hard, Rian following her almost immediately after. Sloane had never felt so alive. Not only had she come to see Rian for who he truly was to her, but he loved her.

Rian loved her.

12

Sloane rolled over, facing Rian as he slept with a hand resting on her bare waist. Her gaze crept over his features as they lay together. His dark hair fell dishevelled over his forehead, the strands only just missing his closed eyes. His long lashes fluttered as he slept. She reached out, tracing a finger along the stubble of his strong jawline.

Rian cracked his eyes open at her touch.

"Good morning," he said, pulling her closer until their bodies were flush. "I could get used to this."

Their lips met, a lazy-morning sort of kiss that left promises for more.

Sloane drew back and smiled. "What did the gifts mean? The key, the White Willow and the word Hawkins? Is the last one really just your horse's name?"

Rian laughed, shaking his head. "Hawkins is sort of to do with Hawk, but not like you think. I'd rather not tell you what any of them mean," he replied, sitting up. He reached for his trousers, tugging them on, then followed with his boots.

"Why not?" she asked. Her gaze narrowed at him despite the pleasant view she was getting of his toned back.

He grabbed a shirt, slinging it over his shoulders, then turned as he buttoned it up. He leaned towards her with a mischievous glint in his eyes. "Because I think it would be better to show you."

"Show me?"

He nodded, then pressed his lips to hers. The kiss was too brief, and she shivered when they broke apart.

"We'll need to find you some clothes first."

"Right," she replied, blushing. "My dress is probably still hanging over the horse's back." She frowned, making to rise. "It was my mother's, and I left it outside all night. I probably destroyed it."

"Wait here," he said, striding towards the door. "It might not be ruined."

"Not like I can go anywhere," she sang, cuddling further into the blankets despite her guilt over the dress.

She was completely naked. Thankfully, Rian didn't live in his family home with his parents and sister. The morning would have been extremely awkward if he did. Instead, he lived in the dwelling beside the stables. It wasn't a big space, but it was private.

"It's still wet," Rian said, returning inside. He lifted the dress to his nose. "Smells a bit horsey, too."

"Great," Sloane groaned, peaking over the blankets at him.

Rian lit a fire in the hearth and laid the dress on a chair before it. "It will take time to dry, but I can think of a way we can pass that time." He winked, unbuttoning his shirt again as he made his way over to her.

"Hmm," she tapped her chin, a smile spreading on her face. "I wonder what you have in mind?"

Sloane squealed when he fell upon her, laughing until he

smothered the sound with a kiss.

"I need to go to the apothecary," Sloane said, slipping into the now dry dress. She'd spent a good while passing the time with Rian, not only in the bed but in the bath too, and now she was all too aware of her absence at work. "There will be customers, and I've already been away for too long."

"Annabelle can deal with it," Rian replied, helping her with the dress's ribbons at the back. "She'll be fine alone for the day."

Sloane pursed her lips. He was probably right. Wait … she spun to face Rian. "What about my father?"

"Do you need to check on him?"

"No," she shook her head. "But you didn't say he would be working at the apothecary with Annabelle. You said she'd be alone."

Rian cupped her face and ran a thumb over her cheek. "I know he doesn't work there anymore, Sloane. I know you run the business."

"How?"

"I'm there every day, remember? I don't know when the last time was that I saw your father other than through a window into your home or the occasional glimpse of him in your garden."

She pouted. "You never said anything."

"I was waiting for you to tell me when you were ready."

"Women aren't supposed to run businesses."

"And it's a stupid rule. You have always been more than capable of running the apothecary."

Sloane wrapped her arms around him, pressing her face into his chest. Tears threatened to fall, but she held them at bay. Rian had known the whole time and hadn't told a soul. He saw her as qualified and had accepted her reasons for not telling him about her father, all without knowing what they were.

She hadn't been the only one keeping secrets, though.

She lifted her head, looking up at him. "Still planning on showing me what the clues meant?"

"Of course," Rian smiled. His hand ran up and down her back. "Let's go."

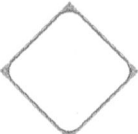

Sloane sat atop Hawk, nestled between Rian's arms as they rode along the dirt track. Her legs dangled on one side, Rian's embrace being the only thing stopping her from falling off. She leaned her side into his chest, loving the feel of him so close to her as they rode. She could have fallen asleep she was so at peace.

"See the White Willows?" Rian asked, drawing her from her relaxation to gaze ahead of them.

She could see the trees in the distance. They were growing larger with each step Hawk took. They were beautiful trees with green and white leaves that created a mesmerising canopy that drooped towards the lush green ground below.

"Is this where you get my orders from?" Sloane asked, thinking of the deliveries Rian had made to her.

"No, this part is the Kline property," he replied. He steered Hawk from the main road up a winding dirt track that passed through the trees. Rabbits ran out from their hiding spots, darting away from the sound of the horse's hooves. "There is another owner further up where I get yours."

They travelled a little further before a cottage came into view. The walls were made from stacked stones of various shades of grey, and the roof was covered in ivy that dangled over one side. Lavender grew beneath the front windows, where its little purple flowers were already in bloom.

Rian halted the horse and dismounted, reaching up to grip Sloane's hips and help her down.

"Is this your house?" she asked, staring at the cottage in awe. It was beautiful. It looked like something from a painting brought to life.

"It was my grandparents," he replied, his hands still on her hips. "After they passed, my father and I started working on repairs. My grandparents would never let us when they were alive, which is a shame, but what could we do? They were stuck in their ways."

"You've been fixing it up?" She raised a brow. "When have you had the time?"

"It's been a slow project," he said. "But I'm almost done; that's why I sent you the key."

She pulled the key out from around her neck. "This is the key to your house."

"I would have told you sooner about how I felt, but I wanted something to offer you that was more than a single room adjoining a stable on my father's land. I wanted to show you that I could be more than that."

"Rian…"

"I don't deserve you," he said, tucking a stray strand of her silver-blonde hair behind her ear. "But I will work every day for the rest of my life to at least try to be deserving."

Sloane's eyes filled with tears, and her bottom lip trembled as she looked up into his eyes. "I'm pretty sure I'm the one who doesn't deserve you."

He cupped her face and wiped away her tears with his thumbs before leaning down. His lips pressed against hers, and he kissed her slowly, as though they had all the time in the world. How was it that he had been in front of her face for so long, and only now was she truly seeing him?

They broke apart, and he smiled at her, taking her hand and leading her up the path. "I want to show you our house."

Sloane's heart fluttered at his words.

Our house.

Nothing had anything ever sounded so perfect.

He stopped at the front door and pointed to a wooden sign above it that had a name freshly painted on it.

Hawkins.

"It was my grandmother's maiden name. We found the sign at the bottom of a trunk when we were cleaning up. She must have brought it with her when she married my grandfather. So, we gave it a fresh coat of paint," he told her. "She came from money. But she left it all to be with him. At least everything but the sign and the key."

Sloane lifted the golden key from around her neck. "This was hers too?"

Rian nodded and indicated the keyhole. "Try it."

Sloane became filled with excitement as she put it into the lock and turned it, hearing a loud click.

They walked across the threshold together and Rian toured her through each of the rooms, showing her the repairs he'd made and the alterations he and his father had done to make it suit the two of them. There was space for their interests and entertaining friends, a sitting room that overlooked the willow trees by the river, and a bedroom at the back with views of the hills in the distance.

"It's perfect," Sloane said once they returned outside. She stared up at her new home from the front steps in awe. It wasn't a large house, but it was theirs, and she loved it.

She loved him.

Sloane took his hand and smiled up at him. "I love you."

Rian matched her smile, the sight brighter than the sun. He stepped closer and leaned forward to press his forehead to hers. "I love you too."

13

Sloane managed to tear herself away from Rian long
enough to visit Emma. As much as she wanted to stay
wrapped in his arms, she had some explaining to do
after leaving the dinner in such a rush the previous night. Not to
mention that she was eager to tell her friend all about how the
night had taken a turn.

As she stood before the gate of Emma's home with the sun
warming her back, she stared up at her friend's open window.
The curtains swayed with the breeze, yet there was no sign of
Emma.

Nerves danced in Sloane's stomach. She really didn't
want to knock if Emma wasn't home. The Charter family were
never unkind, but Sloane had always preferred to avoid them,
nonetheless. They had an air about them that made her anxious.

Eventually, working up the courage, as she had been forced
to so many times before, she pushed open the gate and made her
way up the path. Flowers blossomed in the gardens where bees

buzzed around to collect their nectar. Sloane tried to focus on the insects' buzzing wings rather than whom she might find on the other side of the front door as she finally reached it.

With a deep breath, Sloane knocked, waiting only a moment before the door opened and was faced with Emma's father. Mr Elliot Charter was an intimidating man, and rightfully so. He held a lot of power in Devotion and was well respected.

"Sloane," he said in his deep voice.

She offered him a smile. "Mr Charter."

"How is the apothecary?" His gaze ran over her, analysing. This was one of the things Sloane found nerve-wracking. It wasn't that she thought he was judging her or looking down on her, but over the years, she'd learnt that the man had a habit of assessing everything in his life.

"Well," she said, placing her hands behind her back. "Business is good."

"And your father? I haven't seen him in a while."

"Very busy making remedies and experimenting with developing new ones."

He raised a brow, and she had a feeling he knew she was lying, though he didn't say as much.

"I—"

"Sloane!" Emma exclaimed. Bursting passed her father and knocking him to the side, she grabbed Sloane's hand and dragged her inside. "Tell me everything!"

Sloane laughed, glancing behind her to see Mr Charter let out an exasperated sigh as he adjusted his coat. "Good to see you, Sloane."

"You too," she replied, following her friend upstairs to Emma's bedroom. It was double the size of Sloane's room, with an adjoining private bathroom and large closet. The furnishings were luxurious, the bedding was soft, and everything was neatly put away, likely thanks to the maid.

"So…?" Emma prompted as they sat on the bed. Sloane felt

herself being absorbed into the cushions and often wondered whether sleeping in Emma's bed was like sleeping on a cloud. "Don't make me wait any longer."

Sloane grinned at her friend and then began to recount the last twenty-four hours, at least most of it. There were, of course, some details she wanted to keep between her and Rian. Emma listened intently, only breaking her silence to sigh happily or squeal in excitement.

"It was Rian all along," Sloane said, finishing up her story and grinning at her friend.

"That's so romantic," Emma sighed, flopping back onto her bed.

Sloane laughed, joining her, and the two of them lay side by side, staring up at the canopy above them. Emma took Sloane's hand, interlacing their fingers as they lay in silence. For a moment, they simply enjoyed each other's company and the happiness they were both experiencing in their lives.

"What do I do about Nevan?" Sloane asked, breaking the silence. She bit the inside of her cheek.

"I can ask Connor to break it to him?"

Sloane shook her head. "I should tell him. It's the right thing to do."

If she were in Nevan's position, she'd want to hear it from him.

"You're a better person than I am," Emma chuckled.

Sloane rolled onto her side to face her friend and said, "I don't think that's possible."

Sloane approached the manor on horseback, riding up the bush-lined path. She would have asked Emma to borrow a carriage, but she thought it would be best to avoid encouraging another group event, especially with what she had to say tonight. An audience was not needed.

The sun was yet to set, and the orange glow looked like a halo behind the manor. Sloane dismounted at the front steps where the stone building loomed over her, and a shiver ran down her spine, despite the day's lingering warmth. She ignored it, excusing the sensation as nerves. Explaining to Nevan that her heart belonged to someone else would be awkward, but Sloane felt it was the right thing to do. She wouldn't allow him false hope any longer than necessary.

The large wooden doors opened slowly, their hinges creaking as she ascended the steps, and she found the man in question standing in the doorway with a wide smile on his face. Beyond him, the house was set in an eerie shadow.

"I wasn't expecting a visit from you," Nevan said in greeting. Her stomach squirmed at the delighted look in his eyes. Why did he have to look like that and make this all so much more difficult? "I went by your apothecary, and you weren't there. I was starting to worry. I'm happy you're here. Come in."

Nevan took her hand, leading her inside his large house. He was dressed impeccably as always; a dark blue coat over a grey shirt and black slacks, with the obsidian snake pinned to his lapel.

"Sorry for the impromptu visit," she said, glancing around the hallway. There were no artworks on the walls, no furnishings or possessions of any kind. Maybe he hadn't had time to make the place a home yet. He'd only been in Devotion a short time. "There's something I want to talk to you about," she said.

"You can talk to me about anything."

"Good," she replied, though his eagerness for her to talk to him didn't help the situation.

Nevan brought her into what she assumed should have been a sitting room. There was a sofa and a circular table set before it with a cluster of burning candles and some books atop it, but other than that, the room was bare.

"What have you come to tell me?" he asked, gesturing to the sofa. He placed his hand on her back, guiding her to sit, then took up the spot beside her.

"You see," she started, then took a deep breath and let the words spill from her mouth. "The thing is, I know I have given you the impression that I am interested in a possible romantic relationship with you, and I thought I was initially, but I have come to realise that my heart resides elsewhere. I am so sorry for giving you false hope. I thought I wanted to be courted by you; I really did. It turns out I was mistaken. You are a nice man, and I'm sure one day someone will make you very happy, but that person is not me—"

Nevan's smile turned into a scowl. He rose to his feet, adjusting his coat; the pin with the obsidian snake sparkled as it caught the candlelight. "I tried to do this the easy way, but you have left me no choice."

Sloane frowned. "Excuse me?"

"You could have been happy as my wife," he replied, looking down at her. "You could have been afforded all the luxuries my station would have given you in exchange for one simple thing."

"What?" Sloane asked. She scrunched her brow.

"I want to own you."

"I'm a human, not an object for you to possess," she said, raising her chin. Her heart beat wildly in her chest as she rose to her feet and stood her ground.

"No, but you are a Maker," he replied, stepping towards her. "And we both know that you are no ordinary human."

This caught Sloane off guard. What did he mean by that? "I have no idea what you're talking about."

He shook his head. With each step he took toward her, she took one away from him. "Yes, you do. I came here for a reason; I came here for you. The world may have forgotten who your family is, but there are some who know what happened to Valmenessia." He tapped his serpent pin. "Who know what you are."

"I—"

"Stop lying to me."

Sloane's back hit the wall as he caged her in.

"It won't save you."

"Are you going to kill me?"

He shook his head, running a finger down her cheek. His expression was villainous in the flickering light. "What a waste that would be. No, I want your magic."

"I don't have magic. Only the people on Valmenessia do. You should go there; I'm sure you'd find someone to teach you how to be a Conjurer."

"And be stuck there for the rest of my life if I want to keep magic? When everyone has power, no one does. Outside of Valmenessia, I will be the most powerful person in existence. You have magic, Sloane, whether you are aware of it or not, and I am going to wield it through you."

This didn't make any sense. She thought maybe he was speaking in metaphors. Magic didn't exist outside of Valmenessia; it had to be a metaphor for something else. "I won't marry you."

He looked at Sloane, contemplation written in his features and perhaps sadness too. "No. That deal was taken off the table when you came here to reject me. Even if you agreed to it, I could never fully trust you. So now, you will simply be my prisoner."

"No." Sloane tried to retreat further, but her back was firmly pressed against the wall.

"No?" He tilted his head to one side. "Do you know what happened to the last person who said no to me? She was some stupid woman who I'd thought was you initially. A mistake on my part because, knowing you now, there is no comparison between you and her.

"I laid eyes on her during my carriage ride into Devotion

and she looked the picture of a Conjurer like in the stories. Dishevelled and a mind that was off with the Alvs. When I spoke to her, it only added fuel to my suspicions. I asked her to ride in the carriage with me, and she refused. Something about a husband and children."

"Melanie," Sloane breathed.

"I didn't catch her name, which was a mistake, I can admit. I should have asked. It would have saved me a lot of time," he said, his hand wrapping around Sloane's wrist. His hold was bruising as he dragged her from the room. "Your last name is Maker, after all. I saw where the woman ran home to, and I took her that same night."

"What did you do to her?" Sloane demanded, trying to pull herself from his hold, but it was no use. They descended a narrow set of stairs, and with the light fading, she had to focus her attention on not tripping.

"She's still here," Nevan replied at the bottom. He dragged her along a darkened passage, their footsteps thudding against the stone floor. The stench of bodily fluids filled Sloane's nose, and she had to force herself to breathe through her mouth.

Sloane bumped into Nevan as he pulled to a stop, and her eyes went wide at the sight before her. A sconce burned on a pillar, illuminating the cell beyond the bars, where Melanie sat inside. The woman had been missing for a couple of weeks. Her body was curled against a wall, but Sloane would never forget the eyes. Melanie always had the bluest eyes she had ever seen.

The bars creaked, and Sloane was shoved inside through the iron door. She stumbled to the ground, and her hands scraped painfully on the stone as she braced herself. Behind her, she saw Nevan looking eerie in the flickering light. He smiled wide, then turned on his heel and left, leaving the two women alone.

"Sloane? Is that you?" Melanie croaked.

"Yes," Sloane replied, turning to face the woman. "I'm so happy you're alive. I was worried about you."

Sloane hurried to Melanie's side. The woman flinched and Sloane shuffled back, her gaze running over the woman in the limited light. "Are you hurt?"

"You need to be careful. He will come back," Melanie said softly. "He's always so angry."

"Did he hurt you?"

"His anger has to go somewhere," she replied, hugging herself. "He caught you, too?"

Sloane nodded. "Although, I think I entered his trap more willingly than you did."

"He kidnapped me from my bed in the middle of the night," Melanie said, a sob escaping her. "My kids ... and my husband ... they have been without me for so long. I don't even know if they're alright."

"They're fine. Heartbroken but safe. We'll get out of here," Sloane said. "And you'll be back with them in no time. I promise."

14

S loane had dozed off against the stone wall. Her back
ached from the cold and awkward angle, but it wasn't
the soreness that woke her.

"Wake up," Nevan said, running a baton over the metal bars.
The sound rattled Sloane's brain, and she groaned, clutching her
head. He pointed at two bowls he'd placed on the dirty floor.
"Breakfast time."

Nevan watched her with keen eyes as though assessing a
prized animal as she moved to pick up a bowl. She handed one to
Melanie before getting the other for herself. The contents were not
warm and had no smell. Not bad nor good, and looking at it in the
poor lighting, it was hard to discern what it was at all. Porridge?
A flour and water paste? Something else entirely? Nevan's gaze
remained fixed on her, almost burning in its intensity.

She looked up at him and saw a smirk tugging at his lips.
"Don't eat it all at once."

"What is it?" she asked, looking between him and the bowl.

A frown creased her brow.

"Breakfast," he replied simply, then turned to walk away.

"Wait!" Sloane shouted, dropping the bowl to the floor. Despite it tipping, the contents remained inside. She rushed to stand before the bars with her hands clasped around the cool metal.

He approached, stopping close, too close, which showed just how much of a cocky asshole he was. Sloane wasn't trained in anything other than working at the apothecary. She had no skills in fighting or manipulation. Nothing that would warrant him to believe she was a threat.

And that belief was her advantage.

"What do you want?" he asked, his gaze firmly on her face.

"Are you planning to leave me in here?" she asked as she slowly lifted her hand. "How can I do what you want me to if I'm stuck in this cell?"

"First," he said. "You'll learn to be obedient, and this cell will teach you who you belong to. Then I'll put you to work."

"I'll never belong to you," she hissed, slamming her hand into his chest. Her hand clasped around his snake pin, and as he pushed her off, she took it with her.

"In time," he hissed, brushing down his coat. His hand only just missed the unnoticed torn fabric. "You will break."

With that promise, he left.

Sloane didn't move until she could no longer hear any sound of his presence, then turned to Melanie, waving the pin.

Melanie peered at her with wide eyes. "Is that?"

"His pin." Sloane grinned. "We're getting out of here."

Sloane quickly set to work. Shoving her hands through the bars, she pushed the pin into the lock of the door and twisted.

Nothing happened.

She tried again and again until her frustration had her tempted to throw the stupid snake pin across the room.

"Let me try," Melanie said, coming to her side and holding

her hand out.

Sloane nodded, handing it over.

"My eldest has a passion for lockpicking," she said as she pressed herself against the bars. She pushed the pin into the lock and wiggled it. A click sounded. "Little thief." The door swung open, and Melanie covered her mouth with her hand, her body shaking as tears fell down her cheeks.

Sloane placed a hand on Melanie's shoulder and squeezed, excitement running through her. "You're going to see him again very soon."

The two women ran from the cell along the passage, pausing at the base of the stairs to listen out for Nevan. When they couldn't hear anything, they slowly crept upwards.

Daylight peeked from above, becoming brighter the further they went, and soon they were standing in the bare hallway.

"Where is he?" Melanie whispered in Sloane's ear.

"Maybe he went out?" Sloane suggested, though her gaze was alert as she looked around them.

"I haven't gone anywhere." Nevan stepped out from one of the rooms ahead of them. Sloane's heart raced as he blocked the front door and their escape.

"Well, we can't stick around," Sloane said, shoving Melanie in the opposite direction. "Run!"

They took off down the hallway, and Sloane prayed there was another way for them to get out; a servants' entrance or back door. She would even climb out a window if she had to. She chanced a glance behind her and saw Nevan in pursuit.

"Split up!" Sloane shouted, and Melanie darted left whilst she went right. As she'd predicted, Nevan remained on her heels instead of going after Melanie.

Relief filled Sloane. She may be trapped, but at least Melanie would get out.

She rounded a corner, eyeing a bright light that was pouring through an ajar door. She raced towards it and found herself facing a room walled by windows with a magnificent view of the hills and trees beyond. She reached the door leading outside and pushed down on the handles, desperate to be free, but found them locked.

Nevan's arm encircled her waist, hauling her backwards. "Good try," he snarled into her ear.

Sloane refused to go weakly. She thrashed against him, using whatever power she had to get out of his grasp. Her legs swung in the air, and she made contact with something that gave her enough leverage to force Nevan to stumble backwards.

They both fell to the floor. Seizing the opportunity, she tried to crawl away from him, only for Nevan to grab her and spin her onto her back, where he straddled her. Sloane's arms were immovable beneath him. He pulled at a handle from his coat pocket, clicking a button, and a hidden blade slipped out.

"Enough," he commanded, pressing the blade to her neck. "Don't make me hurt you."

"Too late," she spat. "Just kill me. I'll never do what you want."

"You will," he replied. "You and your father are the only living Makers, the only magical beings outside of Valmenessia. Your father is aging and senile, but you, Sloane, you are young and will give me what I want. You will wield magic for me, and I will become the most powerful man the world beyond Valmenessia has ever seen."

"You're delusional! Magic doesn't exist outside of Valmenessia! And even if I could do magic, I wouldn't do shit for you!

"You will because you are a woman and your duty is to the man of the house!"He snarled, his blade pushing into her skin, drawing blood. "Now stop ly—"

Nevan was thrown sideways, his blade rattling to the ground. Melanie stood breathing hard above Sloane and dropped the wooden bucket she'd been holding.

"Are you okay?" Melanie's gaze ran over her.

Sloane nodded. "You?"

"I will be," Melanie replied, picking up the blade.

She grasped it in her hand and lunged for Nevan. A mirror image of the position Sloane and Nevan had just been in. Melanie straddled him as she drove the blade into his chest.

Over.

And over.

And over again.

Blood splattered her clothing and her face, but she kept going. Even after Nevan lay still, she didn't stop. Not until Sloane wrapped an arm around Melanie's shoulders and carefully took the blade.

"You're okay," Sloane whispered, holding her tight. "He can't hurt you anymore."

15

The fire crackled in the hearth, warming Rian's small home. Sloane nestled into his side, feeling safe and at peace in his arms. She never wanted to leave this spot on the sofa ever again.

Except, of course, to move into their cottage, that is.

A week had passed since the ordeal with Nevan, and Sloane was done thinking about it. She didn't want to let him into her thoughts anymore. There was too much good in her life to dwell on that insane asshole.

He'd thought she had magic.

The idea was laughable, though she hadn't told anyone of his wild notion of how he wanted to use her supposed magic to make him all-powerful. There was no point telling anyone. It was nonsense that belonged in her father's books. Better they believe he was just a disgruntled noble who snapped when he didn't get what he wanted from women.

"Sloane."

She tilted her head, looking into Rian's eyes.

"Are you hungry?"

"A little," she admitted. "But I'm so comfy here." She snuggled further into him and felt his laugh radiate through his body.

"You can stay here," he said, beginning to rise from his seat. "I'll get—"

"No, stay with me," she giggled, reaching to grab hold of him only to fall off the sofa. She thumped onto the floor with an oof, landing on her stomach.

"You alright?" Rian crouched in front of her, and she looked up to see the amusement shining in his eyes and a grin on his face.

"Never better," she replied, blowing a strand of hair from her face.

He reached out, tucking it behind her ear. "I love you, Sloane. I'm sorry I wasn't here to protect you, but I promise I will keep you safe from now on. I will be with you for as long as you let me. Until I take my last breath."

Her heart nearly exploded from the warmth in his words.

Sloane pushed up onto her knees, pressing her lips to his and kissed him gently.

"I love you, too."

EPILOGUE

Two Years Later

Sloane gripped Rian's hand as sweat beaded on her forehead. She gritted her teeth, her body alight with pain as she tried to focus on the sunset beyond their bedroom window. There was an armchair before the glass, her favourite spot in the cottage, as it gave her not just a view of the sky but of the willow trees that now held a special place in her heart.

Unfortunately, the sunset's beauty was not enough to keep her mind from what was happening to her body.

"You're doing great," Rian said, moving into her line of sight

All she could do was nod. She had no strength to give to anything else.

The midwife was commenting on something at the end of the bed, occupied by what was happening between Sloane's legs, then looked up and ordered Sloane to push.

Sloane wasn't sure she could anymore. She was so tired.

"You can do this." Rian squeezed her hand. "You're so strong."

She didn't feel strong.

She felt done.

Sloane let out a scream as she pushed, then pushed again, until another scream filled the room. The sound had her heart skip a beat.

All the pain she had felt was a second thought compared to the little voice that cried out for her.

Rian pressed a kiss to her forehead as a bundle was placed on her chest. "You're amazing. I love you so much."

"I love you too," she said through her tears as she looked down at the perfect child.

Her baby.

"They have your hair," Sloane said, glancing up to Rian only to find him nowhere in sight. "Rian?"

She looked around the room, searching for the man she loved so much. The man who had helped her create the most precious thing in the world. The child she held against her chest.

"Rian?"

The midwife said something about fainting, then her baby was taken.

Sloane wanted to cry. She was so exhausted.

By the time the midwife had finished caring for her, Sloane fell back onto her pillows and was ready to fall asleep.

"Here's your daughter."

Sloane cracked open her eyes to see her father approach with her baby asleep in his arms. He sat on the edge of the bed, carefully passing the child to Sloane.

"Where's Rian?"

Her father's face fell, his eyes leaving hers. The action sent chills down her spine.

"Where's Rian?" she asked more forcefully as panic rose in her.

"I'm sorry, Sloane, he is gone," her father said. "Makers love once, and it never ends well."

"What do you mean he is gone?" She shook her head. "He can't be gone. He'd never leave me."

"It wasn't a choice he was able to make."

"No," she gasped. It felt as though someone had their hand wrapped around her heart and were squeezing it tight in their fist while they slowly pulled it from her chest. He had to be wrong. Her father had to be wrong.

"Your mother—"

"My mother?" she sobbed. "This is what happened to her? She died because she loved a Maker? You?"

He nodded.

"Why didn't you tell me?" Sloane asked with tears falling down her cheeks. Her entire being hurt, the pain worse than any physical wound. "You've told me so much about our family, why not this?"

"If I told you, would you have had the child?"

Sloane bit her lip and looked to where her daughter lay on her chest. She was fast asleep and completely unaware of the death of Rian, her father.

Sloane's soul had been broken in two, and it was taking everything she had not to let herself succumb to the overwhelming grief of losing the love of her life.

She was torn between wishing he were here and knowing that if he was, then her daughter wouldn't be. The idea of not having her daughter was something Sloane could not comprehend. She loved her little girl so deeply; the child was a part of her very being.

If only she could have had them both.

"I'm sorry," her father said softly. He shook his head, placing a hand gently on her wrist. "It is our legacy."

"It is a curse."

"Either way, it is what we must endure to protect the world."

"Fuck the world," she said through gritted teeth, her grief fuelling her anger. "I will not let her suffer as I do. I will find a way to end this."

"You would condemn everyone else to their evil?" His eyes were wide though sadness still swam within them. "You would free them?"

"I would burn the entire world to the ground if it meant she would be happy," Sloane promised, holding her child tight. If death is what kept the Maker legacy alive then death would end it. She didn't know how, but she would find a way. "There is nothing I wouldn't do."

Sloane didn't like thinking of Nevan Grim, yet she found his voice in her head at that moment. He'd said that she had magic, that Makers had magic. She'd never believed him or her father's tales, but now there was proof.

Heartbreaking, devastating, proof.

Rian. Her love. Her life.

Her father's grip tightened. "Sloane, you are grieving. You don't mean that."

"I mean every word." She looked her father in the eyes. Her words were as unwavering as her will. "We have paid enough."

THE STORY CONTINUES...

Find out what happens to Sloane in Vice and Verity,
Book Three of the Valmenessian Chronicles.

Haven't read the main series yet?

Start today!

THE VALMENESSIAN CHRONICLES

Alta: A Valmenessian Novella

Liars and Light

Rise and Reverence

Maker: A Valmenessian Novella

Vice and Verity

Also By Rebecca

The Terrulian Trials

By Chloe Hodge and Rebecca Camm

A Sky of Storms

A Forest of Fire

A Sea of Secrets

A City of Smoke

A Desert of Despair

A Kingdom of Conquerors

I'm a daughter of House Jupiter, the empire's most powerful family built on the backs of those brainwashed to serve.

The king is dead, and the Terrulian Trials have begun. This is my one chance to be crowned ruler of the kingdom and right my family's wrongs.

If only it were that simple.

The House of Ascension isn't for the fainthearted. I must survive three deadly challenges to secure my place as queen—and that's not counting the Potentials ready to stab me in the back.

It doesn't help that four sinfully good-looking guys keep messing with my head. I can't trust anyone, least of all myself.

There can only be one sovereign … and I'll stop at nothing to win these vicious games.

The Terrulian Trials is a steamy urban fantasy series brimming with mystery, magic, and blood. This is a "why choose" novel, meaning the heroine ends up with multiple love interests. This novel is recommended for readers 18+ and is book one of six.

About The Author

Rebecca Camm was raised in Melbourne by a single mother who encouraged her passion for reading and all things magical. She has been writing stories since she was a child to help manage her anxiety and make sense of the world.

Rebecca strongly believes in the power stories have in changing lives. Just like her, Rebecca's characters are flawed, yet they are continually learning. Unlike her, they are confident, witty, and just generally more exciting.

Rebecca lives with her husband and two children. When her children allow her free time, she is either writing or attempting to conquer her ever-growing tbr pile.

Stay in touch!

Website rebeccacamm.com

Newsletter rebeccacamm.com/contact

Instagram @readingwritingdaydreaming

TikTok @readingwritingdaydream

Facebook @readingwritingdaydreaming

Facebook Group facebook.com/groups/rebeccacammsreadergroup

www.ingramcontent.com/pod-product-compliance
Lightning Source LLC
Chambersburg PA
CBHW031949130726
47904CB00012B/1025